Billingshurst's Heritage
A Short History of a West Sussex Village

Compiled by
Geoffrey Lawes

Peacock Press

Map of North end of Billingshurst High Street 1877

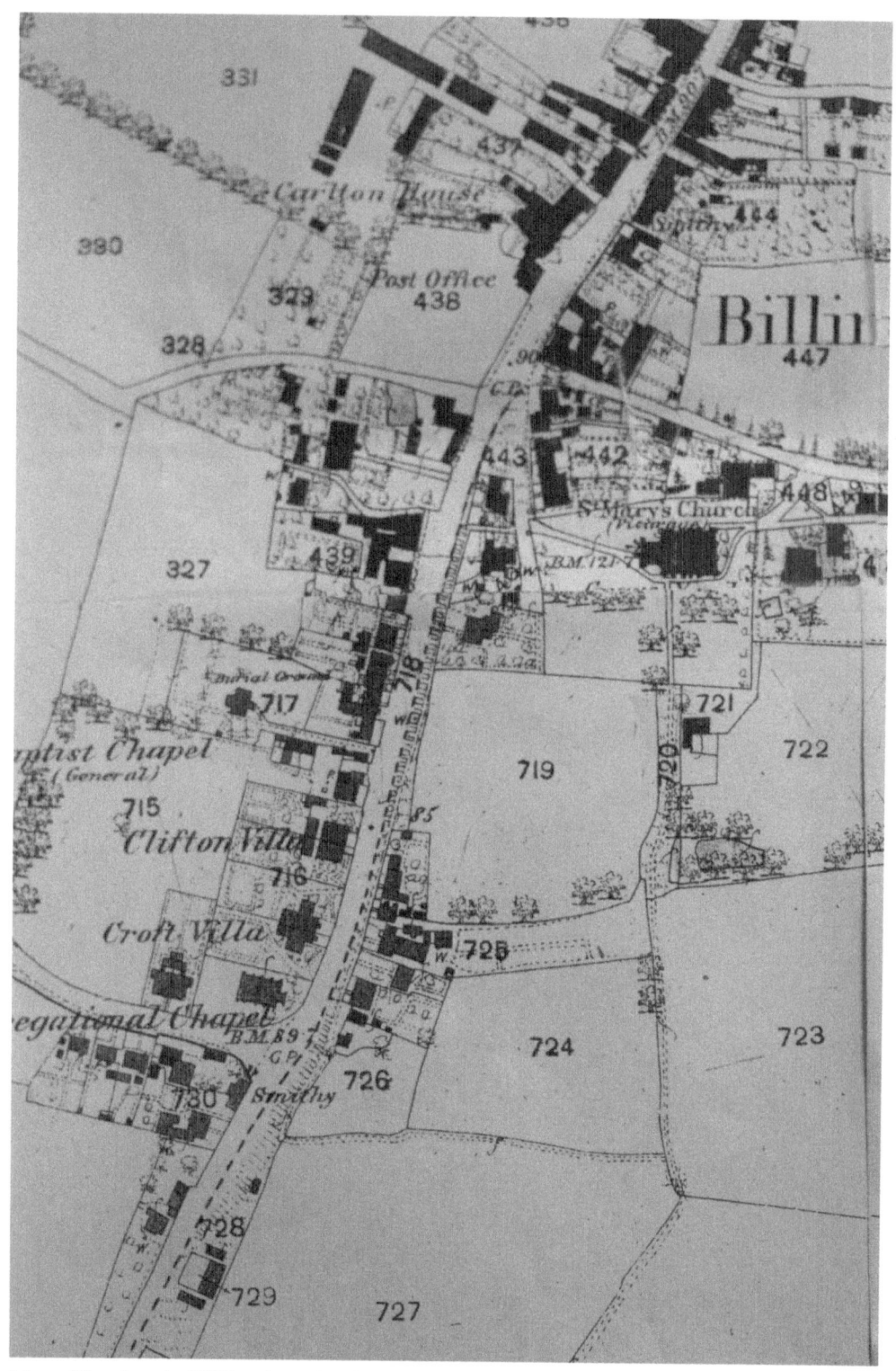

Map of South end of Billingshurst High Street 1877

High Street. Gingers House and Maltings, now the entrance to Jengers Mead

Billingshurst's Heritage
A Short History of a West Sussex Village

Compiled by
Geoffrey Lawes

Village sign at the Community Centre

'There is nothing that more divides civilised from semi-savage man than to be conscious of our forefathers as they really were, and bit by bit, to reconstruct the mosaic of the long forgotten past'.

[G.M. Trevelyan]

Billingshurst's Heritage
© 2012 Geoffrey Lawes

All rights reserved. No part of this publication may be reproduced, stored in a retrieval system, transmitted in any form or by any means electronic, mechanical, including photocopying, recording or otherwise without prior consent of the copyright holders.

ISBN 978-1-908904-25-6

Published by Peacock Press, 2012
Scout Bottom Farm
Mytholmroyd
Hebden Bridge
HX7 5JS (UK)

Design and artwork
D&P Design and Print
Worcestershire

Printed by Lightning Source, UK

Contents

Before the 'First syllable of recorded time'.. 1-2
Homo sapiens exploit the planet... 3-5
The Ancient Britons and the valley where they lived.................................. 6-7
The coming of the Romans and their legacy.. 8-11
The Saxons colonise Britain.. 12-15
Saxon farming and later developments in agriculture............................... 16-21
The conversion of the pagans... 22
Fresh pagans threaten – the Norsemen.. 23
More new Christians – the Normans.. 24
Mastering the Wealden forest... 25-27
The 'First syllables of recorded time' in Billingshurst. The Church and local government.. 28-33
Early parish government... 34-37
The Black Death.. 38-39
Feudal management of the County... 40
The Manors of Billingshurst and district.. 41-42
Cocksbrook alias Hammonds north of East Street.................................... 43
Tudor times... 44-47
James I and the Stuarts... 48-55
Civil War. Charles I beheaded. The republican interlude......................... 56
Restoration of the monarch. Charles II and the Church of England........ 57-58
18th Century – the Georgian era.. 59-65
The 19th Century.. 66-71
Queen Victoria was crowned.. 72-76
The Officials of the Parish Vestry.. 77-79
1851 Census – the year of the Great Exhibition in the Crystal Palace in Kensington... 80-81
The Railway Age... 82-84
Schools in Billingshurst.. 85-88
The Victorian regeneration... 89-91
Hard times and good times... 92-96
Death of Queen Victoria – the 20th Century... 97-106
Post-war Billingshurst... 107-110
More recent developments... 11-115
Hammonds House and Hammonds dairy farm and Little Daux.............. 116-118
Possible future developments... 119
Billingshurst Characters and Celebrities... 120-121

The spirit of Billingshurst 122-126

Acknowledgements 127-128

Appendices
1 Housing developments 129-133
2 The end of the Georgian years 134
3 The early years of Queen Victoria 135-136
4 Mid-Victorian Billingshurst 137-139
5 Late Victorian Billingshurst 140-141
6 Early 20th Century 142-148
7 Post WWII 149-152
8 Occupants of Hammonds 153-154

Index 155

Foreword

Geoff Lawes came to Billingshurst in March 1974 to take up the headship of the Weald School - but it seems like he's always been here. Since then he has served the community at many levels. He is remembered by his colleagues and former students; he has served the Horticultural Society; he has contributed wider service as District & County councillor. He has published on the history and development of the Weald School and on beekeeping.

We are told that when bees have found a good source of pollen they fly back to the hive and make a "waggle dance" to tell the other bees where to find it. This book may be Geoff's dance - it started as an account of the place in East Street where he lives but he soon discovered more nectar. It may encourage others to forage.

This book reveals Geoff's love of knowledge "for its own sake" and displays his natural talent as a raconteur and teacher. Who better then to present a history of Billingshurst?

John Hurd, Billingshurst, October 2012

Billingshurst's Heritage

Introduction

It is natural enough, as we tread the paths around our houses and turn the earth in our gardens, to ponder on what manner of men and women once trod those same paths and sowed seed in that same soil. How did those people earn a living; how did they lead their lives? What pressing business filled their waking hours? What have they left behind for us to enjoy; what were their names and who are their heirs who still carry their genes?

Prompted by such an impulse to find out more of the street where I live, East Street in Billingshurst, I gathered together information from authoritative local historians, jotting them into a notebook. Almost every house proved to have a story and posed a further question. I had originally focused on just one 17th century building, 'Hammonds', my immediate neighbour. But those further questions inevitably led to a wider delving into the research findings of other authorities until the notebook took the shape of an embryonic history. The vista widened from the story of one house to the whole street, which contained the 13th century church, the former workhouse, the old school buildings and other ancient houses with widely divergent histories, together with the echoes of some other notable premises, now long gone. Inevitably a study of the people of one street could not for long be divorced from their interactions with the rest of the village community, nor did it make sense out of context with the geography and history of the wider Sussex region. Consequently a concentric pattern grew from the Hammonds nucleus, and the result is a little book, *Billingshurst's Heritage*. A fortunate factor that made the enterprise manageable was that this is an area remote from the coast, sheltered before Saxon times by ancient forest and not blessed with rich soils, so that it has been protected from intrusion, aggressive agricultural development and industrial exploitation until quite recent times.

The jottings began as a chronological 'line of time' to allow a reader a sense of the evolution and progress of Billingshurst through the passing of the centuries. This time-based mode of presentation has remained as the basic structure of the village story as told here. It proved the simplest way of recording 'gobbets' of information, yarns and anecdotes which are not part of a general topic, and also the names and doings of particular people.

Interwoven among the chronological detail, are occasional essays on major themes which span long passages of time such, for instance, as the development of farming, the evolution of parish government and the provision of schooling.

Ever since man-like primates began to modify the face of the planet, human beings have dictated the superficial features of the landscape. Accordingly this account reaches back briefly to those aspects of pre-history that scholarship and archaeological research have revealed to us. Conversely, at the conclusion it seemed appropriate to speculate on what may lie ahead for our successors who inherit the living space for which we are but briefly the custodians.

Geoffrey Lawes, October, 2012

Before the 'first syllable of recorded time'.

We have to assume that Billingshurst was no different from the rest of what are now the British Isles in offering living-room to *Homo sapiens* and probably to even more primitive hominids from the very earliest times.

500,000 BC

On the evidence of findings at Boxgrove, north-east of Chichester, on a land surface subsequently covered by a gravel beach, our earliest predecessors in the Middle Pleistocene period made flint axes in order to butcher wild animals like rhinos, lions, bears, wild horses and deer. This was *Homo heidelbergensis*, the common ancestor of the *Neanderthals* and *Homo sapiens*. The ones we know about lived on the former beach surface of a great lagoon at the foot of a former chalk cliff during a warm inter-glacial period when the old silt beach stood high relative to the sea. When the glaciers returned to the north the land sank and the waters returned covering their leavings in the silt with gravel and outwash debris from the falling cliff, so preserving a rich archaeological record for us to find in the early 1990s.

These were probably some of the earliest hominids in Europe and it is most likely that they made group sorties in search of meat all over what is now Sussex. They had not yet made fire, had nothing recognisable as a language but were brilliant axe tool-makers and fashioners of spears. An iron-stained axe labled 'Rowner' exists from this time. Subsequently glacial episodes interrupted developments in this Palaeolithic, or Old Stone Age period. It is important to grasp how extensive was that aeon of time; half a million years! Equally we must remember the long sequence of radical changes of climate, sea levels, geology and landscape that occurred in that half a million passing years.

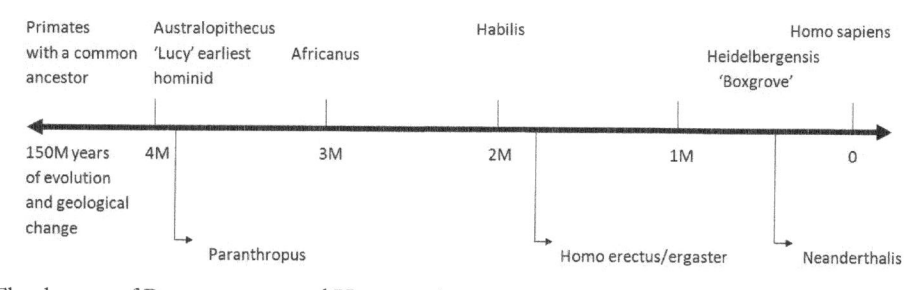

The descent of Boxgrove man and Homo sapiens

500,000 years was but a moment when compared with the 150 million years that preceded it when the underlying sedimentary rocks were laid down and then bent up into a great arch, only to be weathered away, leaving us the chalk North and South Downs and the Greensands and clays that outcrop between them.

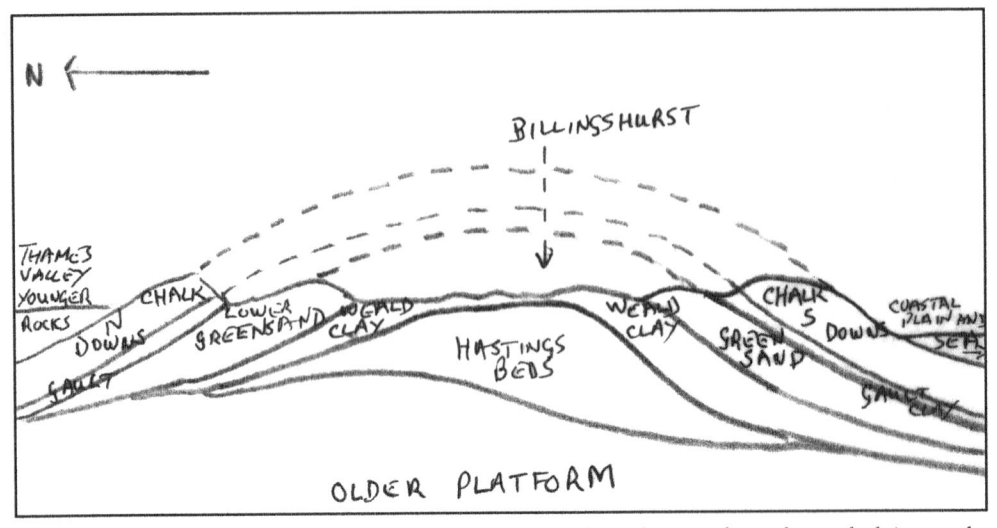

A North-South section across the denuded Weald anticline showing how the underlying rocks outcrop at the surface

40,000 BC

Neanderthal people were living in southern Britain some 40,000 years ago in what is now Pulborough. There is recently revealed evidence of occupation at Beedings Castle off Nutbourne Lane on the greensand ridge. They left behind several craftsman-like flint tools in Hampshire, Kent and elsewhere, notably beautifully made 'boute coupe' hand axes. They succumbed however and were superseded by Cro-Magnon man, the true *Homo sapiens*, also hunter gatherers and nomadic in lifestyle, but sophisticated enough to sew skins, catch fish and wear jewellery. They had discovered the benefits of fire.

Homo sapiens exploits the Planet

6,000BC

From 12,000 BC, after the last ice-age, termed the Neolithic, or New Stone Age, climate change had altered the western European landscape into treeless tundra. *Homo sapiens*, by then, were hunting for the meat of deer and wild horses. In the period from about 8,000 to 3,000 BC, known as the Mesolithic, 'Doggerland', the land bridge to mainland Europe, was finally flooded by rising ice-melt and 'Europe was isolated'. Meantime in Iraq and Palestine quite sophisticated people were constructing the earliest buildings. There is much evidence that New Stone Age people were living in the Arun valley. A site at Okehurst, on sandy ground overlooking the Arun, shows occupation in a pit dwelling and the flaking of flints for at least 2000 years, longer than the present village has existed.

5,000BC

Socially developed people, recognisably 'modern' humans were known to have flourished as far north as the Orkneys in 5,000BC.

From then onwards the climate warmed, trees grew and boar and aurochs (cattle) entered the diet. Dogs and pigs were domesticated, horses trained to work. Sheep wool was made into cloth. There is much evidence of stone-age people living in the Billingshurst area. Local farmers are known to have gathered knapped flints turned up by the plough and a ground greenstone axe. They may well have been the tools brought in by hunters from the south in search of deer meat and skins. Flint flakes have been found in Daux Wood and Clevelands.

Axe heads found at Wisborough Green

4,000 to 2,000BC

The Neolithic time lasted from before 3,000 to 2,000 BC. This is the period of cave-dwellers and the rise of farming for sustenance – but not of dinosaurs. They were living a mere 150 million years earlier! Fred Flintstone deserves an Oscar for the most enjoyable anachronism of retro-science fiction. This is the era of henges, monuments and stone circles. Industrial flint mining was carried on at Cissbury, north of Worthing. There were flint mines at Blackpatch and Harrow Hill north of Angmering where excavations have revealed antler and ox shoulder-blade tools, flint axes, lamps and galleries. It was the dawn of religion, and massive public works like Stonehenge. There is much evidence that such people lived in Billingshurst, especially in the river valley.

Excavated flint pit at Harrow Hill showing galleries.

To 700BC

The Bronze Age lasted from 2,000 to 700 BC. That era is associated with beaker pottery, turned on a wheel, metal culture, using gold, silver, tin and copper and with long barrows and cremation urns and an economy based on mixed farming with livestock. Billingshurst had middle Bronze Age people dwelling locally on the evidence of five axes found 'near Hammers Farm' in the 19th Century, said to be in the British Museum. Bronze, a mixture of copper and tin, made stronger tools. In this era the greatest innovation of all time, the wheel, which was discovered in Sumer (modern Iraq), came to Britain.

The Ancient Britons and the valley where they lived

200AD

It is probable that our whole area was by now covered by the as yet unnamed Wealden Forest, so any settlement would have been beside the local stream, feeding the River Arun which runs for some miles along the boundary of the present parish. Billingshurst lies in a broad valley, or better a three-sided basin, at the confluence of small streams rising from low clay hills to the South, East and North. Those streams met together, the main one running along what is now the High Street. Then it would have been a sparkling stream among the trees, but it now runs in a culvert, hidden from view since the beginning of the 19th century. It was once called the barrel drain, probably because barrels were used to create it. Water drained in from ponds in the Jengers area on the West, and off Billingshurst Hill to the North. The main feeder ran along the bottom of the steep sided Bowling Alley to the North East draining the area later called Cocksbrook. The water course then joins the Parbrook, again from the East, rising in the area round Great Daux running on the north side of Daux Avenue and now piped to the brook alongside Natts Lane It then flows west forming a tributary of the Arun.

Hills to the North East form the watershed between the Adur and the Arun rivers at 120 feet above sea level, only a short distance beyond the East Street Hill. Places as close as Summers Place, Wooddale and Rowfold Grange drain northwards to the River Adur.

Any villagers then would have been 'Ancient Britons' speaking a Celtic language not dissimilar from Welsh, Gaelic and Breton. It is an open question whether they were really a Celtic race who had invaded from Gaul. The working of metals evolved into smelting and forging of iron tools and weapons – the Iron Age. Warring tribes developed. Those in our region were the Atrebates. These tribes had a King or Queen, nobility, middle and working classes and slaves. They built hill forts like The Trundle where many lived, worked and trained for warfare. They worshipped local gods and animals, the Druids, their priests, setting great store by human and blood sacrifices to appease their gods.

The geology of West Sussex dictated where earlier people chose to live. The loamy soils of the area round Chichester, extending eastwards to Brighton, gave the best farming opportunities to in-comers, and the chalk downs, together with the gault clay and greensand belts north of the scarp slope offered a welcome to successive invaders, much friendlier than the dense woodlands and intractable clay of the Low Weald. Iron Age Celts, Romans, Saxons and initially even the Normans chose to live and work on the 'Champion', as the favoured area is known.

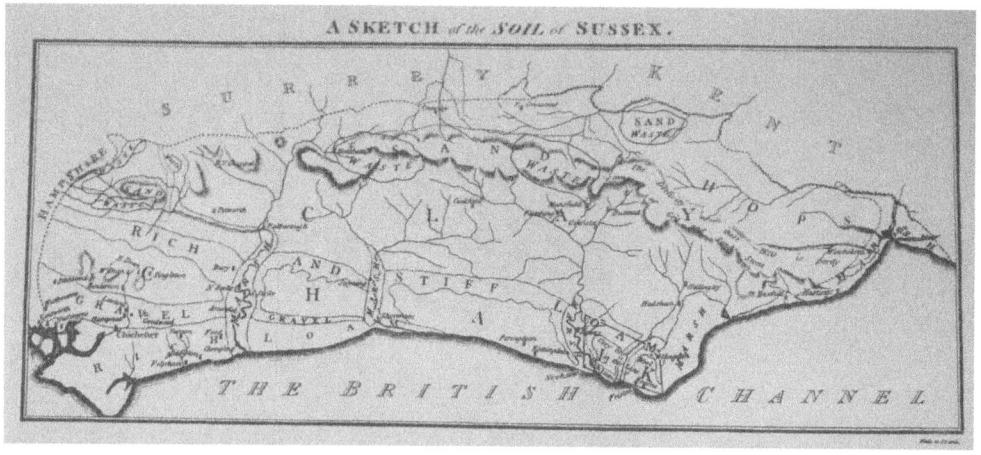

Sketch of 1813 showing the soils of Sussex, better in the south than in the Low Weald clay around Billingshurst.

To 43AD

The Belgae, a tribe from Belgium, arrived on the Manhood peninsula from 200 to 43 BC. Much of the rest of Britain was now a patchwork of forest and fields where tillable land had been exploited by clearing the trees. Our Billingshurst district would have remained largely dense woodland, since the trees and shrubs that flourished in the clay and the absence of firm roads in the winter mud created a formidable forest barrier. The English Oak, known as the 'Sussex Weed' (Quercus robor) dominated the flora. Just to the north iron ore seams might well have given rise to some deforestation though the earliest known iron workings were in the High Weald of eastern Sussex. Daux Wood remains as the closest descendant we still have of the original natural ancient Anderida Forest. To the south, Chanctonbury and Cissbury evolved into forts at this time.

Billingshurst's Heritage

The coming of the Romans and their legacy

43AD

The Roman Emperor, Claudius, profiting from knowledge of Julius Caesar's failed invasions of 54 and 55 BC, which had been ruined by bad weather, sent 40,000 invading troops to the south coast of Britain. They had the willing cooperation of the King of the Regnenses (the realm from Dover to Chichester) named Togidubnus who was one of the Belgae. He later became Tiberius Claudius Cogidumnus. Thus a tribal chief was enabled to build a spectacular palace at Fishbourne as a reward for his connivance in the subjugation of most of Britain as part of the Roman Empire. The Britons, speaking Celtic, would have been obliged to understand some Latin to stay on good terms with their Roman masters.

45 to 470 AD

The Romans established extensive settlements on the coastal plain at Noviomagus Reginorum, (meaning 'New Market' which became Chichester), Fishbourne and at Bignor. They built the straight road we now call Stane Street (A29) as a post road link to Londinium. The nearest Posting Station, for resting and changing horses is just South of Pulborough at Hardham with another North at Alfoldean (Roman Gate). The first necessity of a conquering colonial power is the ability to move military forces rapidly over the subject territory in order to suppress rebellion by such as Boudicca and to challenge enemies at the borders, like the Picts and Scots. The road itself, however, shows little evidence of military fortification. By creating Stane Street and subsequent extensions in all directions from Londinium the Romans achieved their security and access to the metal ores and other benefits that their client state could provide.

That very road left a legacy on the economic and cultural landscape of Sussex. All subsequent roads were orientated in parallel, up to London and down to the coast, essential both for defence and for trade. The Romans did branch out eastwards from Stane Street, towards Lewes, at Hardham for example, in order to exploit iron ore in East Sussex. Generally, however, East-West routes were rudimentary and not developed. Even today only two major roads traverse the south of England, shadowing both the North and South Downs. The third route, the A272, linking East Sussex and Hampshire which crosses Stane Street at Billingshurst might well have given a nodal importance to the village were it not for the fact that it did not exist until recently. East Street merely petered out.

Most of the drove roads of Sussex mimic Stane Street in direction if not in straightness. Though there was one extending westward from Billingshurst towards Wisborough Green, a larger village than Billingshurst, one must assume that there was no significant trade on an East-West basis to call an important highway into being. Even the surviving railways echo the 'coast up to London' pattern initiated by Roman Stane Street. The lack of communication, east and west, no doubt as a result of the daunting forest barrier, has been proposed to explain the late arrival of Christianity to Sussex from Kent and Wessex where it flourished.

There is scant evidence of Romano-British settlement at Billingshurst other than that associated with Stane Street itself, a possible Roman brick recycled into the Church tower, some 2nd century coins including one of Marcus Aurelius (161-180 AD). Stories of findings in a field at Five Oaks have not yet been investigated. The Romans are said to have brought plums, walnuts, roses, mulberries, vines, leeks, garlic, cabbages, mint, parsley, and, regrettably, ground elder to England but it is unlikely they planted anything in Billingshurst. There were, however, extensive gardens at the Palace of Fishbourne.

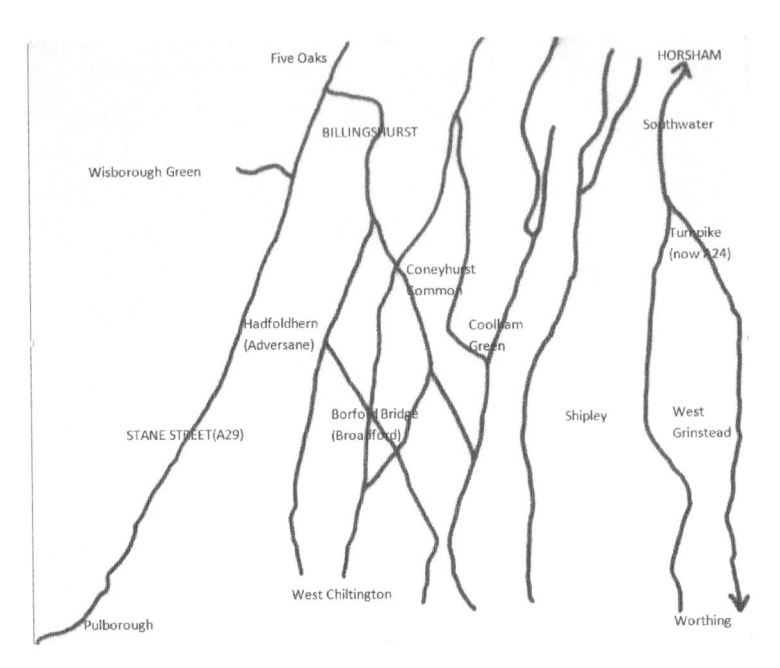

Sketch showing the old droving roads to the east of Stane Street from a map of 1795.
No road then ran eastwards beyond Coolham.

367 AD

As Roman power disintegrated at home, so marauding bands of Saxons were able to infiltrate the south coast of Romano-Britain, as they did elsewhere. But Romano-Britain still flourished. (Bignor Villa was built for example) until the incursions of 367. Christianity had reached Roman Britain around 300 AD under the Emperor Constantine.

The Saxons colonise Britain

To 477 AD

By 410 AD Rome had been sacked by the Goths, the last two Legions of Roman troops were withdrawn from Britain and the end of the Roman domination was inevitable. The incoming Saxons (or Germani) would occupy whatever settled sites they found and mingle with the Romano-Britons in situ, using them for labour in return for protection.

Aella came to Sussex. He was a pagan, worshipping Odin, King of the gods, Tiw, Woden, Thor and Freya (hence the names Wednesday to Friday). His son Cissa gave his name to Chichester. Roman buildings fell into ruins. The so-called 'dark age' of the Saxons began when they started on the work of opening up the wilderness of the Wealden Forest, beginning by 'turning the valley bottoms into water meadows, the forest margins into arable and pasture'.

477 to 1066 AD

The Saxons, benefiting from the Roman road, cleared enough forest on fertile alluvial soil beside the streams to begin the village near what is now Lloyds Bank. Pulborough, which reached as far as Scats Country Stores and Newbridge with Rowner Mill, was then far more important, figuring in Domesday Book of 1086.

Billingshurst means 'a wooded hill of Billa's people' implying the knoll just up the A272 where the parish church stands. ('Bill' - head of a family, 'ing' - of the people, 'hurst' - wooded hill) The likelihood is that it was a small family settlement, not yet a parish or community, headed by one 'Billa' of indeterminate origin, rather than a populous Saxon tribe. The village was probably too poor and undeveloped to deserve to be named in the Domesday Book though Horsham does not appear either. However it has been established that manors near the south coast utilised the acorns and other fruits of the woods growing in the heavy local clay for fattening their pigs. Parts of Billingshurst and Horsham therefore appear in the Domesday assessment, but only as outlying parts of their 'parent manors'.

The dwellings would most likely have been simple structures made by lashing three or more poles together at the top to form a conical circular or oval framework, then roofing it bottom to top with turf, bracken, straw, clay or other handy materials. Hovels of this nature, or of only slightly more permanence, were the dwelling places of the ordinary people of Billingshurst until quite recent times. For many centuries the common people would, at best, live in humble, impermanent timber-framed, single storey, chimneyless dwellings. The fine oak-framed buildings that have come down to us were all built for yeoman farmers or other gentry.

The residual Celtic speakers, many of whom had no doubt migrated westwards to Wales or Cornwall out of reach of the Saxons, would have been obliged to speak a new tongue, now named 'Old English', the language of the epic poem *Beowulf*. Few would have been capable of writing and certainly none in Billingshurst. *Beowulf* begins:

Hwæt! Wé Gárdena in géardagum	Listen! We --of the Spear-Danes in the days of yore,
þeodcyninga þrym gefrúnon·	of those clan-kings heard of their glory.
hú ðá æþelingas ellen fremedon.	how those nobles performed courageous deeds.

Ordered by Alfred the Great, the 'Anglo-Saxon Chronicle' of 848AD is in similar Old English.

The Saxon people of Billingshurst would have only one name such as John or Alfred. Surnames came in quite slowly with the Normans. To distinguish people more exactly a second name might be attached from the place where they lived such as Greenfield, Coxbrook or Hurst. John and Tom might have sons named William Johnson and Walter Thompson. Another distinction could be based on their occupation such as Cooper, Smith, Wright and Carter or from a nickname, usually based on physical characteristics like Small, Sharp, Little and Long.

It is likely that boar, wolves and bears still roamed the forest as well as the deer, foxes and badgers and squirrels, then the red kind, which still survive. All wolves were cleared from England by Henry VIII's time. The Normans brought in the rabbits, kept in warrens for food and skins. The name Coneyhurst, meaning 'rabbit wood', implies that they were kept there.

Caedwalla, ruler of Wessex (685), and his successor Ine, became the local king of the area when he annexed Kent, Surrey and Sussex. It was then that the administration and system of law in divisions known as rapes and hundreds was devised. In return for protection the common people of Anglo-Saxon England were controlled, exploited for tax, rent, labour and military service by their tribal betters according to their holding of 'hides'. A Ceorl, or 'free' peasant farmer, typically had one hide of land. The Normans adopted and adapted the rapes to their own feudal purposes. Control was exercised through sub-divisions of land, the Manors, from the 'tun' or major administrative centre – in our case, Arundel.

Ultimately there were six Rapes in Sussex, Chichester Arundel and Bramber in the west and Lewes, Pevensey and Hastings in the east. The Rape of Arundel, granted to Roger de Montgomery in 1067, was the oldest and largest. He owned 83 manors. The Rape of Chichester was established from it in 1250, but the Rape of Bramber also dates from the 11th century, created from the Rapes of Arundel and Lewes. It was granted to William de Braose who controlled 38 manors.

Part of Speed's map of 1610 showing the Rape of Arundel

The responsible officers for each Manor were the Steward and the Reeve. The latter was a kind of foreman, estate agent and accountant to the Lord of the Manor and the ruling hierarchy. This basic administrative structure was systematised and defined by the Normans to facilitate their tax income and ensure their military defence. Geoffrey Chaucer depicts typical characters of Manorial England in *The Canterbury Tales* as they had evolved in the 14th century – monk, nun, friar, parson, the man of law who was a magistrate, the Knight, who might have been Lord of many Manors, with his Squire and a yeoman forester servant, the self-serving reeve, the cheating miller and, at either end of the social scale, a rich Franklin, (a freeholding farmer), and a poor ploughman. By Chaucer's time the French and English languages had coalesced into the Middle English tongue and the Saxons and Norman people had merged into the English people without national distinction of social class. Chaucer exemplifies, in particular, that most cherished of English characteristics, a broad sense of humour.

By 1066, through constant warfare, England had slowly evolved into a single state, under the leadership of Wessex. Seven kingdoms had emerged on a regional and tribal basis, known as the 'heptarchy', comprising Wessex, Sussex, Kent, Essex, Mercia, East Anglia, and Northumbria. All but Essex had kings who, at some time, were accorded the role of Bretwalda, or 'overlord of the English Kingdoms'.

1. Oak framed 17th century Yeoman House, Southlands at Adversane

2. Stout Sussex Oak beams at Southlands carrying the chamber above

Saxon Farming and later developments in agriculture

The three Rapes of West Sussex are parallel North-South slices of territory with an inherent economic geographical logic. Each had a coastal port, a river, a defensive fort and a share of the better coastal soils, the Downs, the greensand belt and a hinterland of the backwoods of the Wealden forest. This North–South orientation is echoed in the Drove Roads which, in our area can be traced along seven distinct lines, all running more or less parallel to Stane Street.

They are normally over thirty feet across, and, where metalled, have wide verges. When they wind through the greensand hills to the south, they narrow into deeply cut trenches where sand and sandstone have been excavated and passing herds have eroded the soil. There are about fifteen such roads detectable in West Sussex. They probably originated in Saxon times or even earlier and were fully exploited after 1066. Their purpose was the driving of stock back and forth to take advantage of woodland forage in season. Pigs were reared and fattened by rooting among the oaks for acorns and for beech mast and chestnuts, a practice known as pannage. The pigs' snouts helped clear the forest by disturbing the topsoil, breaking off saplings and the dense undergrowth. Many manors on the coastal plain had inland outposts of property reserved for this purpose. Ferring with Fure in Billingshurst is a prime example as is Climping with Clemsfold. Wherever the suffix 'fold' occurs in a place name, like Rowfold, Alfold, Slinfold, Kingsfold and Polingfold we can suspect some such north-south manorial linkage. (Old English 'falod' meant an enclosure for domestic animals).

Today livestock are carried in lorries, but up until Victorian times, pigs, cattle and sheep were moved on their own four legs, or even two in the case of Norfolk turkeys! Traffic along these roads ran from the Horsham area down to the lusher pastures and water meadows and more populous regions north of Worthing. There were the recognised links between coastal manors and their 'backwoods' properties One drove road passes round Billingshurst and runs due South through West Chiltington. It is reasonable to speculate that, bearing in mind the simple dwellings of ordinary people, the early drovers would, temporally, move their dwelling places as well as their stock, whether they were the owners of the livestock or slaves or serfs employed by the tribal hierarchy. Dogs would have been trained to keep the animals under control. It was a kind of Wealden transhumance.

In 1256 the Bishop of Chichester, who was the Lord of many Manors, kept a moated stud farm at Drungewick, just north of Billingshurst, with 250 oxen, 10 bulls, 100 cows, 3000 sheep, goats and horses. Scrawny mediaeval oxen were but half the size of modern cattle and some would be slaughtered at Martinmas for winter meat as would the hogs. The meat would be salted to preserve it. Pike, tench, carp, perch and bream were kept in the stews, or fish ponds of Manors and doves in their cots. Carp were fed with pease and grew to 14 inches in four years. Bacon was the main meat meal of the moderately well-to-do and cheese the protein of the serfs, eked out by rabbits, thrushes, larks and larger game, caught or poached as opportunity offered. Impassable roads in winter would discourage the cultivation of arable crops to be marketed in distant towns. The sticky soils would have limited the growing of cereals to what was needed for subsistence. At the time of Edward III (c 1350) it was recorded: 'At Billynghurste in the Rape of Arundel...60 acres of land...worth 2d an acre and no more, and is of no value to sow, 'propter magnitutinem bosci', [close by great woods] but the pannage when it happens is worth 10s'.

Geoffrey Chaucer, in *'The Knight's Tale'* written about 1382, has given us a list of native trees, being used in his story to build a funeral pyre, that might have been found in Billingshurst woods at that time:-

"...ook, firre, birch, aspe[n], alder, holm, popler,
Wyllugh[willow], elm, plane, assh, chasteyn[chestnut], lynde[lime], laurer[larel]'
Mapul, [black- and haw-]thorn, bech, hasel, [y]ew, wipple-tree[dogwood]"

He omits elder and crab apple, but includes 'holm' which in Middle English meant 'holly'. Chaucer was retelling a story of ancient Greece when holm-oaks were revered, but that species did not come to England until Elizabethan times. Chestnut probably came in with the Romans. There are said to have been 110,000 sheep in Sussex in 1340. Red Sussex beef cattle, originally with white forward pointing horns were held in high esteem in the 18th century. They are believed to be refined descendents of original Wealden stock. South Down sheep are small but were celebrated for their wool as well as the texture of their meat. A man was expected to sheer fifty sheep a day in summer, hard work with hand-held clippers.

1. Sussex Cattle

2. South Down sheep

Much of England in the 15th century and through to Tudor times enjoyed an economic boom from the production and export of wool. This prosperity has left us a legacy of superb churches in East Anglia and elsewhere and the symbolic Woolsack upon which the Chancellor still sits. It is likely that the rich medieval farmers on the Champion would have shared in the bonanza and the Drove Roads would have been used to take advantage of pastures in the summer which had been won from the forest. The soils of the coastal plain, the chalk Downs and the greensand belt would have been preferable for wintering and spring lambing. The cold Wealden clay in winter would lead to foot-rot and other troubles though the shaws and woods offered the possibility of shelter.

It is probable that our earlier Billingshurst farmers would have kept their beef and dairy stock mainly for sustenance and as draught animals. Relatively few would have been for sale, driven to market on the hoof. The characteristic large hay-barns beside old farmhouses bear witness to systematic cropping of hay for winter fodder. Inventories made for wills list oats, barley, wheat, peas, beans, vetches and 'tares' for stock which were stored there. Cattle can better withstand the mud and poached earth than sheep. 'Grass upon wet land, corn upon dry'.

The Rev. Arthur Young in his celebrated book on Sussex agriculture of 1813 tells how Sussex oxen were normally bred for plough and haulage work from 3 to 7 years of age, and then fattened up for slaughter when 8 or more. Tractable willing working animals were kept going longer and the fractious beasts went earlier to the butcher. They were essentially dual-purpose animals, broken in to the yoke alongside older beasts at 2+ years. They ploughed in teams of 4 or 6 if the going was good and up to 10 or 12 in heavy soils. Their milk was a secondary consideration, though what the Sussex breed lacked in quantity it made up for in quality, rich enough to yield an average of 5 lbs of butter a week and 30 lbs of cheese a month from the skim milk. It was reckoned that a 100 acre holding of arable land required a minimum of a team of 8 oxen and 4 horses. Up to a third of the acreage would be used up to feed them summer and winter.

Young describes the standard rotation for the stiff clays of the Weald as 1. Fallow 2. Wheat 3. Oats 4. Clover and Grass for two or three years 5. Oats, Pease or Wheat. He deprecates 'fallowing', recommending turnips instead. He thinks much Sussex farming is old-fashioned and is in favour of the new threshing machines which yielded more grain than the flail and saved labour. He also regards shaws as a hindrance to the ripening of corn and poor sources of timber. Imported wood was just as good. The land should not be used for growing ships' timbers. Growing 100 year old oaks for the purpose was a waste of land. "Corn and cattle, mutton and wool, would mark the progressive improvement of the county and the Weald, in lieu of being covered in woods, would smile with plenty and prosperity". As far as the arable soils of Billingshurst were concerned he must have had reservations. Wheat, yielding only 16 bushels an acre, contrasted with 50 bushels on 6 foot straw at Felpham, using his own figures, was a loss-making enterprise, though necessary for bread. Profit came from the succeeding oats or barley and fodder crops.

At Hammonds Farm there is still a good deal of chalk in the old farm yard, clearly brought in more recent times to combat the winter mud where the cattle had to stand. Billingshurst is known at one time to have hosted two cattle fairs held on the Green on 8th November and Whit Monday mainly for the sale of pigs. On 12th September there was another bigger fair held at Hadfolds-herns, now elided into the name Adversane, where horses, cattle, pigs and corn were sold. There was a 'pork roast' in a booth on the Green where two tall posts and a cross beam stood. This feast marked the moment when pork was 'in season'. A fair was held at Shipley on October 21st. Arthur Young concludes that, 'The Weald of Sussex should be a grazing district. Large dairies with butter cheese and hogs; with beef and mutton for Smithfield'.

It would not prove expedient to plough up many pastures for wheat and barley until the coming of the Wey and Arun Canal in 1813, the railway in 1841 and metalled roads in Victorian times. Up till 1813 the Arun had been navigable for freight only as far as Newbridge. 'Timber, plank and all sorts of convertible underwood are sent from the Weald and the barges return with chalk, coal or lime'. During the brief life of the canal this trade was enhanced by the link via the Wey to London. The value of cereal crops had risen sharply in response to the Industrial Revolution, threats of the Napoleonic wars, and the rapid growth of population in the 19th century. Wheat trebled in price in twenty years so remedying Rev. Young's earlier criticism of loss-making wheat crops.

The London-Horsham turnpike began in 1758, giving better access to hungry markets. From then on we find millers and maltsters becoming the leaders of the community as arable farming became more profitable with good prices for corn needed to feed the rapidly expanding towns. The Corn Laws of 1815 protected farmers from foreign competition by tariffs. But until mid-century the high price of bread and low wages had brought great hardship to farm labourers. Things improved for them with the repeal of the Corn Laws. There were soon three malt houses in the village. This period also saw the growth of enthusiasm for gardening and allotments and the keeping of domestic animals, fowls, rabbits, bees and pheasants for sport.

After 1874 however the detrimental effect on arable farming of the repeal of the Corn Laws kicked in when growers could no longer compete with imported grain and meat. This devastated the profit from home-grown cereals so that much arable land reverted to pasture. Only milk, hay and straw could be sold at a profit and land values plummeted. As Wilde's Lady Bracknell put it, 'Land has ceased to be either a profit or a pleasure. It gives one position, and prevents one from keeping it up. That's all that can be said about land'. There was, however, still a market for dairy products.

See-sawing between arable and pasture continued. During the great depression following World War I much land was neglected as unprofitable. However from 1939, with the 'dig for victory' campaign, many meadows went under the plough under instruction from the War Agricultural Committees.

Small fields, characteristic of the Billingshurst district, do not suit well with modern harvesting machines. Post World War II prosperity has encouraged alternative recreational uses such as sports fields and equestrian paddocks and hayfields, at the expense of dairy farms, which have declined in profitability. More controversially many picturesque fields, not lucky enough to be deemed in planning law as 'of outstanding natural beauty', have been developed into housing estates to meet the needs and desires of incomers to the region. Dairy farming at Cocksbrook/Hammonds ceased when the Barnes Brothers retired in the 1980s. The dairy farms of Mr. Morris at Five Oaks and Mr. Voice at Adversane had also closed. Milk floats served the village from Five Oaks until the 1970s from a site now occupied by Civil Engineers.

1. Milk bottles of
Barnes of Hammonds

2. And Voice of Adversane.
The smaller 1/3 pint bottle was supplied to schools, sold at a halfpenny a bottle.

New crops such as linseed, peas and beans, maize for silage-making and oil-seed rape and Christmas trees have brought fresh interest to the summer landscape. 'Diversification' became the order of the day on farms, encouraging such stock as llamas, alpacas, goats, rare breeds of pigs, edible snails, trout lakes and maggots for anglers and local specialities such as cheeses and meats for Farmers' Markets. Utilisation for recreational use is increasing, mainly for horses but also for sports such as at Jubilee Fields in Billingshurst, or golf courses, as at West Chiltington and Slinfold. Setting land aside to promote wildlife along headlands or create environment-friendly parks and refuges is increasingly popular. In the mid 20th century several outlying farms concentrated on broiler chicken and battery-hen egg production in large sheds, but by the millennium more stringent humane legislation and the high cost of fodder and fuel had led to their closure.

We must conclude, however, that most of Cocksbrook would always have been meadowland, as indeed it has remained to this day. The patchwork of small fields was liberally interspersed with shaws and woodlands which not only offered food, but also shelter for stock, and oak timber for building, fuel and a refuge for foxes, deer and game. Coppicing was widely practised for faggots, sticks, hoops and palings. Cordwood was cut for charcoal and oak bark for tanning. Management of the timber assets was an important aspect of the lives of the people. Charcoal is still made locally and logs for winter fuel are readily available. Trading in fencing and timber building materials still prospers.

The conversion of the Pagans

597AD - 681 AD

In 597 Pope Gregory sent Augustine to evangelise the pagans of Kent where Aethelbert, the King, was ripe for conversion. Subsequently Christianity spread throughout the land, and the first churches and abbeys were established. Most surviving early church buildings in Sussex date from the 12th century though earlier wooden structures may well have occupied the same sites. A significant change came in 681 when St Wilfrid made his second visit, beginning the conversion of the Sussex people to Christianity.

It is likely that progress into the forested Billingshurst Weald would have been slow. For that same reason local people would have shared little of the splendid Saxon culture now revealed by the Sutton Hoo treasure in Suffolk, or the educated court of Alfred, King of Wessex, or in the manuscripts of the monks at Lindesfarne. The earliest surviving West Sussex Saxon Churches are at Worth and Sompting [960] and the nearest at Bolney where the South doorway dates from about 900 AD.

Fresh Pagans threaten – The Norsemen

994 AD

Though most of Britain and northern France was constantly under the assault of the Vikings in Anglo-Saxon times, the present-day West Sussex area escaped serious intrusion and was never part of the Danelaw, established after the successful invasion of The Great Army from 866. The coming of the Norsemen had the effect of putting an end to two centuries of warfare between the Saxon kingdoms of the heptarchy. The Billingshurst area would still have been remote and inaccessible to raiders, and to a degree protected by the forts along the Saxon shore and the resistance of Alfred the Great. The Norsemen were defeated by Alfred in the 800s but they were still raping, pillaging and plundering the coastal settlements as late as 994 AD. King Ethelred paid 'Danegeld' to the Danes to get them to go away, but by 1013 England was ruled by Canute, a Dane who inherited from Svein Forkbeard, who had murdered King Edmund Ironside, Ethelred's son. The Norse Vikings had meantime colonised Normandy, so they did eventually rule Sussex and England.

More new Christians – the Normans

The greatest change came after the Norman Conquest of 1066, famously following the death of Harold Godwinson and his army at Battle in East Sussex. The Normans were bloodthirsty militant Christians who subjugated their Saxon predecessors and fraternised with them. They retained the Saxon land divisions and manorial customs, but superimposed their feudal rights, so that all lands ultimately belonged to King William the Conqueror, who parcelled out his properties to his Norman henchmen. The earliest Abbey was built at Battle by 1095, and Chichester Cathedral was resited from Selsey in 1075. Hardham Priory, 6 miles to the South of Billingshurst dates from 1248, otherwise surviving church buildings were from 1300 onwards, as indeed are the very oldest houses of the yeoman farmers. The monastic foundations in West Sussex were generally colonial outposts of mother monasteries in Normandy itself. The Normans built 500 forts throughout England much more quickly to consolidate their mastery. At this stage the integrated community, the 'Vill' or village slowly evolved.

The chief architectural contribution of the Saxons and Normans was their oak-framed hall-houses, many of which still grace our countryside. The 'wrights' sawed green oak into stout beams in saw pits or squared them with axe and adze. When they had cut them to make up a pre-tested, rectangular, jointed framework, the 'frame was raised' on a prepared site on firm footings, pegged with wooden pins and roofed with thatch or stone. Walls were often made of wattle and daub and the smoke from the central hearth escaped through a hole in the ridge, way above. Subsequently windows, chimneys and upper chambers and inner walls evolved, so that all of our old houses have been substantially modified as building technology and fashion dictated. These skills persisted for centuries, eventually being superseded by bricks and bricklaying in the 18th century.

1066

Mastering the Wealden Forest

When the Normans arrived the Saxon Andredesweald was by far the largest forest still remaining in England. The Venerable Bede described it in the 8th century as a region 'thick and inaccessible, the abode of deer, swine and wolves'. Its clearance and settlement for agriculture was a splendid achievement of our pioneer predecessors.

The question is who it was that cut down the trees in the area in and around Billingshurst so as to create the patchwork of small fields and pastures that have come down to us? When were the hedgerows laid to divide fields and mark off property boundaries? Were there, at some point, three fields subdivided into strips as in more fertile and workable soils of England? In the absence of written records we can only assume that most of this work was undertaken under the aegis and at the discretion of the Norman Barons by the Anglo-Norman peasantry by degrees throughout the 12th and 13th centuries. Some 'manorial strips' were cleared at Rowfold even earlier. The local controlling body for land north of East Street was most likely the Manor of Pinkhurst, with its head-quarters and Manor House in what is now Slinfold. Elsewhere in the village were the lands of the Manors of Wiggonholt, Storrington and Bassett's Fee.

By 1650 the farm strips on 'open fields' on the Champion had been enclosed. There is evidence of the 'common field system' on the Lower Greensand at West Chiltington, Ashington and Petworth. This agricultural system prevailed as the dominant pattern throughout England in a wide belt from Dorset north-eastwards to Norfolk, embracing the midlands and north-eastern counties. It led, typically, to the creation of three great fields in a village, divided into strips owned by different people, with further areas of uncultivated common land. Ultimately, and chiefly in the 18th Century, these big fields and commons were 'enclosed' to the benefit of profitable and large-scale productive agriculture and the richer landowners, but to the detriment of the peasantry.

However the heavy Wealden clay east of Billingshurst would not have encouraged development of the three-field system of arable farming. It is much more likely that there was progressive clearance by felling and grubbing up the stumps, known as 'assarting', in order to furnish small pastures of five acres or less. Enormous physical effort went into clearing the underwood bushes, felling trees and burning cut-over patches. The rooting of hogs helped the process but the clearance would have been an arduous pioneering challenge.

So Lower Weald farmsteads, like Cocksbrook would have been fixed when assarting was completed and would remain in that form. Great fields, farmed in strips on a three-year rotation, wheat, barley and fallow, never existed hereabouts and the land was 'enclosed' from the outset. While other enclosed regions of England were making huge strides in cultivation methods, stock breeding, drainage and fertilisation, modernisation and 'improvement' on the Lower Weald was at a standstill. Billingshurst yeomen would have run mixed farms, fundamentally sustaining their families and workers on a local and self-sufficient basis, rather than producing large surpluses to market for profit. The lack of good roads to a market and the intractability of the clay soils offered little alternative.

Draught animals employed would have been oxen. Because of the shape of their necks horses would have been strangled if yoked like oxen. The use of the horse-collar to enable horses to be used as draught animals was still a novelty in the 10th century. Oxen were still used in Sussex into the early 20th century. This very absence of 'improvement', of the clearing of hedges and copses to create profitable estates and accommodate machinery, has left us a legacy of the rich and various patchwork of fields and meadows, lanes, shaws and small farmsteads. It is a unique inherited landscape that is our duty to preserve and cherish.

Landscape historians are agreed that the forest had been colonised and the field pattern established by the time of the Black Death – 1348. Interestingly enough, this is the time when our scanty written record of our predecessors begins.

Characteristic of the area are the frequent 'shaws', some still evident. Many hedges of ancient origin have been narrowed to their present state in recent centuries. When fields were first won from the forest, wide hedgerows were left as divisions and boundaries, a good many of which survive as small woods also known in some parts of the country as 'rews'. Hedges can be dated by the number of different bushes they sustain reckoning on a gain of one new species every hundred years. Studies in Billingshurst have suggested that the most ancient are possibly those marking the boundaries of both parish and manor, such as that between Billingshurst and Rudgwick (12 species), next such manorial divisions as that between Marringdean and Hadfold (10 species) and most recent, in the majority, those managed hedges edging fields possibly planted between 500 and 700 years ago. The oldest hedges may indicate where fields may have been won from the forest by assarting. They were more than just boundaries since they were a valuable source of hazel nuts, blackberries, crab apples, bullaces, damsons and acorns. Blackthorn gave sloes and timber for tool handles and walking sticks. Wide hedges had underwood for faggots for baking ovens and farm use and were rich in birds and other wildlife. They offered shelter for rabbits and game and corridors for safe movement.

With the passage of time the feudal obligations of the peasantry, according to the custom of the Manor, to provide soldiering in time of war, labour in field service when called on and rent in money and kind to their noble Lord, were gradually diminished, but continued to be much resented and the occasion of periodic revolts.

Billingshurst's Heritage

The first 'syllables of recorded time' in Billingshurst. The Church and local government

1215 AD

At the beginning of the 13th century we are at last able to make use of some written records of the ownership of land and 'messuages' or dwelling places in the village. Written documentation of the doings of the ruling classes are of course much more readily available. We know a good deal about King John who confiscated Knepp Castle, which was a fortified hunting lodge, and Bramber Castle and the signing of Magna Carta in 1215. Our sources of information about the relatively unlettered people, living and working in the backwoods, are necessarily more limited.

1. St. Mary's Church

2. St. Mary's Church today

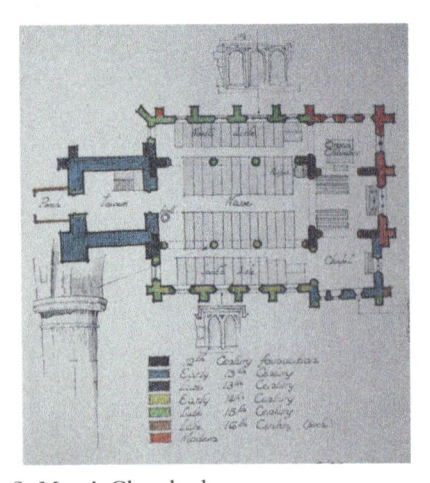

3. St. Mary's Church plan

1274 AD

We do know that the earliest building in East Street is St. Mary's Parish Church. It was begun in the 12th century, possibly as early as 1100 A.D. At first it was under the aegis of the Priory at Arundel. In 1250 St. Richard, Bishop of Chichester, formed vicarages where he thought the monks were neglectful, so the earliest part of the church was built between 1160 and 1200. We do not know which Manorial Lord actually founded the present church. The most likely is de Braose of Bramber.

The first known Vicar was Thomas de Selhurst in 1274. With the dissolution of the monasteries by Henry VIII, the tithes passed to the owners of Okehurst where the Bartellot family were tenants of the Manor of Bassett's Fee. They had acquired it by marriage into the de Okehurst dynasty. They held it till 1579 when it passed to John Wiseman whose daughter married an Edward Goring of the family who became the eventual owners. Edward died in 1617. The Gorings held the Great Tithes until the 1860s when they auctioned it off. Many local Manors were originally church property gifted to the Abbott of Fecamp, a French monastery, so that they had Summers, Duckmore and Okehurst and Rosier. When the king thought it expedient to secure the profits to Englishmen rather than French, about 1450, he simply transferred the rights to a monastery at Syon in Middlesex.

A William Frye (1349) heads the next known list of Vicars. The oldest parts of the present building, apart from a Roman brick, are the 13th century tower and Lady Chapel with its crown post roof. The nave has a 15th century decorated oak-panelled ceiling with 117 carved bosses, fine tie beams and a 15th century early 'wagon' roof and timber framing. The tie beams are some of the oldest in Sussex, if not the most impressive in appearance, cut between 1200 and 1300 and closely resembling many in northern France. The 120 foot 8-sided spire was built on the old tower in the 18th century. It is covered with wooden shingles, originally of oak, but since 1972, of Canadian pine. Score marks on the south wall are said to have been made by medieval archers sharpening their arrows at practice after morning service The Greenfield tombs in the churchyard have interesting epitaphs. That to Samuel' who died 1720 aged 48 reads:

'All you who pass this way along
Think you how sudden I was gone
God does not always warning give
Therefore be careful how you live'.

Another famous Vicar, Nathanial Hilton, who died in 1655, was a stout Puritan so the Catholic images inside had to go! The children of John Downes, who was one of those who condemned Charles I to death were baptised here. John died in the Tower of London and escaped execution on the grounds that he had been bullied into signing the King's death warrant by Oliver Cromwell. He had been MP for Arundel and amassed a fortune from the confiscated royal estates. The Kings Arms is recorded in the Churchwardens' Accounts as having been 'struck out' in 1653, during the Republic, and money paid for 'setting and painting', at the Reformation in 1661.

In 1662 the Act of Uniformity re-established Episcopal worship and there were recriminations. On St. Bartholomew's Day two thousand ministers who refused to give their 'unfeigned assent and consent' to the Anglican service and re-established Book of Common Prayer were ejected from office. Rev. William Wilson, a non-conformist, and father of six sons was among them. He went into hiding and continued preaching at Arundel and Thakeham. He was arrested and had to appear at Petworth Quarter Sessions for continuing to preach, on the hostile initiative of a local magistrate and Thomas Oram, his successor at the Vicarage.

Quakers were particularly vulnerable. William Albury of Horsham wrote: 'Richard Shaw as he was riding jurny was sett upon by two drunken men in the town of Billingshurst and pulled of his horse and one of them drew a sword and swore he would kill him because he was a Quaker...one of these was a magistrates man and his master was in a drinking and would not come out to rebuke his man although word was sent him in that his servant was like to do a murder at the dore'. He also tells how John Pryor and his wife were fined at Petworth Sessions in 1676 for allowing a seditious meeting in their barn at Billingshurst in a manner not 'according to the liturgy and practice of the Church of England'. The informants were Penfold and Cowper and the Magistrates Weekes, Westbrook and Thomas Henshaw.

One Incumbent, in 1863, wrote lengthily to Mrs Botting who was taking over the business of Mrs. Trower's shop, protesting about intrusion on Glebe 'waste land'. Rev. G. Wells, 1792-1823, had made a careful map showing the Glebe Lands, some 13 acres in all, as a record of exchanges of strips of land with Sir Charles Goring to extend the churchyard. It was further extended in 1866 and 1926. However by 1974 the decision was made that there was no room left for more burials and an alternative cemetery has yet to be found.

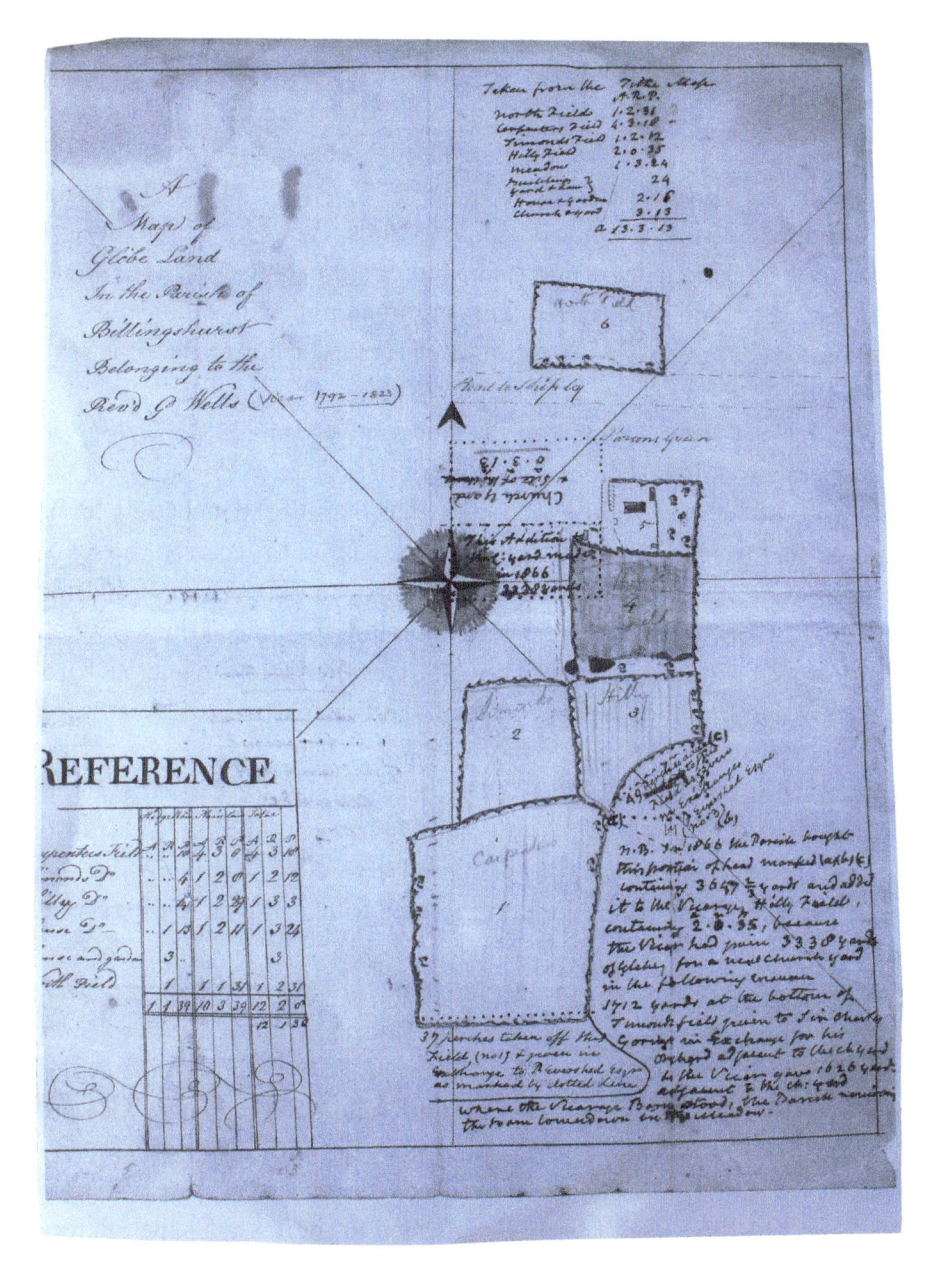

Vicar's map showing Church Glebe

The Vicar's Glebe land was originally extensive comprising most of the terrain East of South Street from Carpenters as far as the National Westminster Bank and also a field beyond East Street now called Rosehill. What is now the Carpenters Field estate occupied the majority of the territory. In 1635 it was recorded that modest rents were paid to the Vicar for the smithy land opposite the Chapel, Churchgate and Brick House on the corner of East Street where W.H. Hubert was the surgeon. Three parcels of land were known to have been sold off. Brick House is where the Nat-West Bank now stands, the so-called Village Green where the Causeway houses stand and space opposite the Chapel, where the smithy stood, now shops, was all leased at a modest 3 shilling annual rent, and it is most likely, a lump sum payment 'in a brown paper envelope'.

John Fuller was a one-time tenant of the Glebe lands. When he went bankrupt the Rev. Beath took the land in hand and farmed it for a time. He exchanged some land with Mr. Evershed, and then retired. He continued to live in Billingshurst as a farmer, until buried here aged 73. The land Mr. Evershed acquired became what is now Station Road.

Cecil Brereton (1886-1890) carried on a business, advertising in the *British Bee Journal*, selling swarms of bees, colonies and queen bees all over England.

There is a brass of Thomas and Elizabeth Bartlet (Bartellot) dated 1499. 'Pray for the sowels of Thomas Bartlet and Elizabeth which Thomas deceased the XXX day of Janever MCCCCLXXXXIX [1499]' of Okehurst, and 17th century alabaster murals showing the Goring family (1617) with five children, three of them infants. Sir Edward Goring received the Great Tithe and bestowed the Living. Richard Luxford is commemorated too. He died in1654 and was married to a relative of Bishop Joseph Henshaw, Lord of the Manor of Bassetts Fee.

E.V. Lucas tells of a 'race which was held every Sunday for certain seats in the chancel and the tactical 'packing' of the same by the winning party.' He also relates that 'a noble carved chair used to be placed in one of the galleries for the schoolmaster [probably Henry Wright] and there he would sit during the service surrounded by his boys'.

Extensive Victorian restoration work was done in 1866 under the aegis of Rev. W.H. Bull and Henry Carnsew, with an architect Robert W. Edis. The result was described by Nikolaus Pevsner as 'rather disastrous'. Among other changes to the arches, two galleries were removed, a new font, pulpit and reading desk were provided, the present Vestry and organ chamber was built and three new east end windows filled with stained glass. Open seats replaced the owners' mixture of private pews. They demolished the school formerly attached to the Lady Chapel. Before 1866 the side chapel was used as a vestry, for Vestry Meetings. Then it moved to the tower. When Mr. Carnsew lost his young wife Henrietta Maria, he dedicated the East widow of the North Aisle to her memory. More recently the organ came in 1883; two new bells in 1897 and in the first decade of the 20th century a fresh pulpit, lectern and communion rails. Another stained glass window was added in memory of James Hall Renton J.P. by Major-General J.M.L. Renton of Rowfold Grange. The church plate includes a cup and flagon of 1631 and alms dishes of 1640. These have the initials of the contemporary Churchwardens on them.

In 1892 Mr. R. Morris of Five Oaks built a Mission Church there near the Inn, now demolished. A similar Mission Church came in 1928 at Adversane both premises being used for social events and meetings.

Modern students of church architecture can find Norman church building features at Wisborough Green, with characteristic round arched doorways built up to about 1180 and some 4' 6" wall, at Itchingfield where the North side of the nave is original Norman, with a round-headed west doorway, and at West Chiltington with wall-paintings and two round-headed windows. The church there dates from the early 12th century. The Church of St. Mary's, Horsham has two Norman doorways.

Early parish government

When we think of a Parochial Church Council today we expect it to concern itself with domestic and administrative matters about the church and churchyard, the congregation and the ministry of the clergy and their assistants. The modern Parson, in crude terms, is an employee of the Church Commissioners rather than the parishioners and has no explicit role in local government.

It is important to remember how much more significant were the Vestry Meeting, and the Incumbent who might have chaired it, in the administration of the parish from the 14th century until the late 19th. The Parish, as an institution, existed in Saxon times, but was fully realised after the Norman Conquest. Then the Lord of the Manor would contribute his tithe for the church building and its upkeep and expect his tenants to do the same, only keeping to himself the right to bestow the living.

By Tudor times the Hundredal and Manorial Courts were beginning to decay. Their administrative powers then passed to the natural successors, the Vestry Meeting. This was, effectively, a parochial parliament. So in the Billingshurst parish records, still preserved, we read not only of the maintenance of the church clock, bells, windows and the shingles on the steeple, but also of payments to maimed soldiers, paupers and children, of work on the almshouses and an emigration fund for people wanting to leave for America and Canada. As regards the church clock, a special 'Clock Field Charity' was set up to maintain it. One resident was alleged to have been guided home by its chimes in a fog and made a deed of 55 shillings a year to maintain it in perpetuity on the security of the Clock Field at Townland. This is probably a comfortable myth disguising the fact that the rents of small parcels of land due to their owners, the churchwardens, were taken in exchange for the pledge to pay an annual sum and to disarm the criticism of non-conformists who always wanted income to be spent on the poor rather than the fabric of the Anglican church. It was a shrewd deal in which valuable plots like the site of the Blacksmith's Arms and Manor House changed hands. In village politics the 'main chance' of private profit was often on the secret agenda. The Vicar Henry Wray Brown (1815-1830) was in dispute with parishioners unwilling to pay him their small tithes. A meeting was held, 'but no business was done owing to the disorder which prevailed'. He is safely buried under the church porch.

The power of the Parish Vestry Meeting to levy a church rate, from early times, led naturally to the administration of other levies, notably the Poor Tax. This was instituted to deal with the welfare of the indigent and the discipline of idlers and vagabonds. At first the Vestries worked in tandem with the Manorial Courts, but central governments, from Tudor times, had continually invested them with ever greater responsibilities. They were expected to look after the arms and welfare of the local militia and to appoint waywardens to attend to the upkeep of the dirt tracks that passed for highways. By nominating and paying constables they had responsibility for keeping law and order. The Vestry Meeting controlled tax budgets and as a result a select group of local notables became, as accountants will, the dictators of parish policy. They collected the rates and were in charge of how they were spent. W.E.Tate describes the parishes as 'miniature republics'. They enjoyed far greater community autonomy than we do today where authority is exercised to only a limited extent by Parish, District and County Councils but in most respects by central government legislation. In those days tax rates were agreed by the Vestry and ratified by the local Magistrates.

One drawback of that system was that worthy persons of a dissenting disposition, of whom there were considerable numbers in Billingshurst, tended to be side-lined. Baptists and Quakers and other non-conformists were not best-pleased to pay their taxes to the established church-goers and their tithes to the Anglican Vicar. By an Act of 1601 all Vestries were enjoined to meet at Easter to appoint Churchwardens and Overseers of the Poor. Non-conformist farmers duly took their turn as such officials.

Yet earlier in 1538, Thomas Cromwell had made Incumbents the Registrars of Births, Marriages and Deaths. They were to keep parish records in a 'sure coffer', secured by two locks known as the Parish Chest. St. Mary's had two of these, the older one of about 1700 containing scales to measure bread and flour. These were most likely churchwardens' tools to use as part of their civic duty to check weights and measures, a kind of 'office of fair trading'. The other chest in the tower dates from the 19th century.

Conscientious Vicars were well worthy of their hire, their financial reward coming from a share of the tithes and the profit of their glebe lands. At Billingshurst 'there is also belonging to the sayd Vicarage a yearely pension of five Nobles to be payd by the parson of the sayd Parish at the Feast of St. Bartholomew'. Tithes were meant to serve three purposes; to provide a living for the Incumbent, the maintenance of the church property and congregation, and the welfare of the poor. The Vicar had to be not only a farmer but also was often, in later times, expected to be the chairman of the Vestry administration as well as the spiritual and welfare guide to the parish flock. Every parishioner of some status was obliged to shoulder a share of civic responsibility, taking turns to be churchwardens. They were legally officers of the Bishop and normally appointed by the parish though under certain difficult circumstances the Vicar could nominate one of them. On one occasion in the 17th century it is pointedly noted that the appointments were 'of the whole parish'. The Vicar did not always get his way.

To supervise the work of the parishes, on behalf of the monarch, there was one constant force – the bench of Magistrates or JPs. They were normally landowning gentry or rich merchants, the 'squirarchy' of England, unpaid and hopefully imbued with the spirit of *noblesse oblige*, responsible for keeping the peace and enforcing justice. They had powers to fix wages and services, license liquor sales, discipline poachers and other felons and supervise the workings of the Poor Law.

These old democratic Parish Vestry arrangements were concluded by the introduction of elected Parish Councils in 1894, and for which there was initially great enthusiasm. Thirty-three people were nominated for election for 13 seats! Of recent years there have been barely enough nominations at the quadrennial elections to match the places available. However, the strict limits of parish income and responsibilities today are in marked contrast with the rights and responsibilities of our forebears. They alone were the 'welfare state', the police force and the administrators of matters now dealt with by central government and District and County Councils.

1894 was the turning point of the process. The caring responsibilities of parishes were superseded throughout the 20th century, notably when District Councils took on that role and even the duty of appointing Overseers was taken away in 1927, a process concluded by the Beveridge Report and the welfare legislation of the Attlee government in 1945.

We should bear in mind, however, that local government in former years, implied heavy local taxation on people with property. Today centralised regulation and social welfare depend on centralised collection, mainly through income tax and VAT. The parish precept is only a small fraction of the rates, collected by the District Council, and mostly spent by the County Council and Police Authority. Formerly income tax was minimal. Mr. Gladstone threatened to abolish it altogether. But the people of Billingshurst who were moderately well-off were faced with bills for Parish Rates, Poor Tax and tithes together with any feudal dues exacted by the Lord of the Manor. It is little wonder that several were rendered bankrupt.

Poor Tax was systematised by the Elizabethan Poor Law of 1601 which required the collection of a parish rate by the Overseers to provide food and clothing to those they deemed deserving. The idle poor continued to get a whipping. From 1662 only settled residents of a parish were entitled to relief. Outsiders were moved on to a place where they had a claim by birth or marriage. Tithes, in particular, were greatly resented, and not just by Dissenters. The Great Tithe on grain, wood and hay was payable to the Rector who was often a layman and an absentee. In the case of Billingshurst it was the Goring family. The Small Tithe, a tenth of everything else produced, such as milk, honey, eggs and vegetables grown on land tilled with a spade went to the Vicar. Payment in kind was abandoned in 1836 to general satisfaction. After that payments were commuted, paid in money as a rent, and by the landlords rather than the tenants. Tithes were not abolished until 1936.

It would, however, be a mistake to regard the autonomy of the parish as an idyllic, self-governing community, always exercising its 'little brief authority' with the best of motives, always addressing itself to the common weal. We may be sure the local worthies, traders and yeomanry, managed affairs to their own best advantage, trimming rates and investing in works to suit themselves. They would, for example, fine people for bringing paupers into the village who might prove a charge on the parish rates. But over and above that, then as now, real authority rested with the monarchs and their ministers, elected by a restricted franchise. These were the power-brokers of society who pulled the levers of control by Acts of Parliament, enforced by the Magistracy and backed by the militia. The Vestry worked within the law of the land, and when national policy changed the local leaders changed with them, after the fashion of the Vicar of Bray.

The Black Death

1348AD

At the Norman Conquest the population of England was about 2 ½ million, rising to about 5 Million by 1300.

However the major social event of this century was the Black Death which swept through England from the west country from 1348 to 1350. Some 1.5 million people died, about a third of the population. About 30 villages in the Downs were deserted. Though isolated, Billingshurst is unlikely to have escaped the death toll. Depopulation had the effect of improving the lot of peasant survivors whose labour, now in short supply, became more expensive to landowners. Our local forebears would have enjoyed progressively greater freedoms from feudal control and more opportunities to take on fields as lease or freeholders. The landowners could no longer rely on field service from serfs to work the land and were glad to commute the service for cash and willingly rented out their demesne to yeoman farmers. It is likely that some farmland won from the forest reverted to scrub following the plague, to be recovered by Tudor times.

In 1381 an unpopular Poll Tax prompted John Ball and Wat Tyler to lead a popularist Peasants Revolt. The rich monasteries and lay rectors who took the tithes of the parish and parson were especially targeted, and there was much resentment of *heriot* where the best beast passed from the dead tenant to the Lord, of *merchet*; a fine on marriage; the enforcement of field work and the costly obligation to use the Lord's mill. The Statute of Labourers had attempted to fix wages when labour was scarce. The rebels captured London and, for a short while, looked to have secured the rights of free men, but brief concessions to placate the majority, followed by brutal suppression of the ringleaders, soon restored the status quo and the domination of the ruling classes. Nevertheless the uproar was such that serfdom withered away in England while persisting in continental Europe. Though Kent and East Anglia were the source of the main antagonists we may be sure there were repercussions in the minds of the people of Billingshurst as news of the rebellion spread.

1381

[The customary administrative divisions as at Domesday (1086) are as follows:-

County or Shire.   Sussex was divided into East and West from the 12th century, but got separate County Councils only in 1888.

Rape   A group of Hundreds, with its own Sherriff. In Sussex it would embrace 40 parishes. Each rape had its own river, forest and castle.

Hundred   An administrative area, originally responsible for law and order, levying troops and raising taxes with its own court. Covered 100 homesteads or 'hides'.

Tithing   An area containing 10 households

Vill   A village

Manor   A major property or land division

Hide   8 Virgates (in Sussex, 4 elsewhere). Between 60-120 acres

Virgate   The land 2 oxen could plough in a season -20/30 acres

Ferlynge   A quarter of a Virgate

The residual powers of these divisions and their courts were seriously diminished in 1867 when County Courts were established, and in 1894 when Urban and Rural District Councils took on local administrative responsibilities.

Feudal management of the County

An important feature of Norman feudalism was their regularisation of the Manorial System. The King delegated control of a rape, at a price, to a Baron, a Tenant-in-Chief. He in turn subdivided his demesne to Lords of the Manors, often dubbed 'Knights', with similar rights and obligations. He often held land, his demesne, 'in hand', the Manor Farm or Grange, and parcelled out smaller holdings to serfs or villeins. They benefited from protection and the legal control of the Manorial Court of law. Some serfs' holdings were 'dependent', requiring military and labour services which were sometimes commuted for cash. Others were 'free' without such obligations, but held on copyhold for a rent. The term originates from the practice of giving the tenant a copy of the court roll as proof of his legal right. Tenure was usually hereditary, subject to a fee on changeover. Villeins' holdings could be sub-let. A village could embrace several Manors and a Manor could reach into more than one parish. Many Manors were gifted to Church Bishoprics and monasteries. Locally parcels of land 'paid suit and service' not only to Pinkhurst Manor but also to the Manors of Ferring and Fure, Bassetts Fee, Wiggonholt, Dedisham and Storrington. The parish of Billingshurst had several Lords of the Manor within its boundaries. The Bishop of Chichester owned Ferring with Fure. He was a major landowner of a strip two fields wide across the width of the parish including Woodhouse and Fewhurst. The Village Parish, which was the creation of the church, outlasted the Manors, which were legal property holdings deliberately created by the Normans.

The Manors of Billingshurst and District

The focal point of this history is an old building near the end of East Street called Hammonds. Hammonds Farm, alias Cocksbrook, is in the County of Sussex, the Rape of Arundel, originally held by the Norman Tenant-in-chief Roger de Montgomery, the 'Half-hundred' of West Easwrith and is part of the Manor of Pinkhurst. Roger, a senior commander at the time of the Battle of Hastings, was also gifted estates in Shrewsbury where he chose to live and die. While there he confronted the Welsh and won the land now known as Montgomeryshire. There is a hamlet in the cheese and apple region of Normandy, the Pays d'Auge, East of Caen named Sainte-Foy-de Montgommery where General Rommel was strafed in 1944 by one of Bernard Montgomery's airmen! A remarkable coincidence of names. It is quite near Falaise where William the Conqueror was born and the hamlet of Camembert, and the town of Liverot, a land of big cheeses.

Roger is said to have earned his magnanimous reward at the crucial Battle of Hastings. Here is one account of his part in the battle which depicts the mettle of the man and the violence of the struggle for England as depicted in the Bayeux tapestry. It is called 'The Story of the Saxon Knight':

'William sat on his war-horse and called out Rogier, whom they name de Montgomeri, "I greatly rely on you. Lead your men hitherward and attack them from that side!....The ground thus pointed out for the charge was the steepest and most difficult part of the hill....but Roger and his division did their work gallantly and were the first to break through the English stockade. Roger himself had a hand-to-hand encounter with a Saxon champion.... he wielded a Northern hatchet with the blade a full foot long and was well armed ....being tall, bold and of noble carriage. In the front of the battle where the Normans thronged most, he came bounding on swifter than the stag, many Normans falling before him and his company. He rushed straight upon a Norman who was armed and riding on a war horse and tried with his hatchet of steel to cleave his helmet, but the blow mis-carried, and the sharp blow, glancing down the saddle-bow, driving through the horse's neck down to the ground, so that the horse and rider fell together to the earth. The Normans were about to abandon the assault when Roger de Montgomerie came galloping up with his lance set, and heeding not the long-handled axe, which the Englishman wielded aloft, struck him down and left him stretched upon the ground. Then Roger cried out, "Frenchmen strike, the day is ours!"

Unfortunately other records show that Roger was still in Normandy at the time of the battle, looking after William's interests. He had contributed soldiers to the invasion force and was handsomely rewarded.

Billingshurst's Heritage

Much of Billingshurst was in the Manor of Bassetts Fee originally held by the Abbot of Fecamp. The Manor House in the High Street, an old timber-framed house erected in the early 18th century, now with a Georgian facade, was the main site. Henry V gave that Manor to the monastery at Syon in Middlesex. Wm. Garton was bailiff in 1535 and his son Francis bought it from Queen Elizabeth I. It subsequently passed to the Henshaws (1603-1690). Joseph Henshaw was a prominent divine, who became Dean of Chichester and Bishop of Peterborough. Philip Henshaw however is described as a lunatic. The ownership then passed by marriage to Bartholomew Tipping, then to one Collins, Thomas Clear and Maurice Ireland. Other Manors in the neighbourhood, creating a patchwork pattern of ownership, were Storrington, Wiggenholt and Ferring-cum-Furehurst.

In the Pinkhurst Court Roll of as late as 1872, we learn of the Lord of that Manor and his Manorial team:- 'The Court Baron of the most noble Bernard Edward, Duke of Norfolk, Hereditary Earl Marshal of England, Dewdney Stedman, Gentleman, Steward of the Manor, and Thomas Clear, Reeve'.

On the evidence of local history, of Messrs. Clear, Garton and Henshaw, the position of Manorial Reeve, Bailiff or Steward, was a sound rung on the ladder of wealth and social advancement.

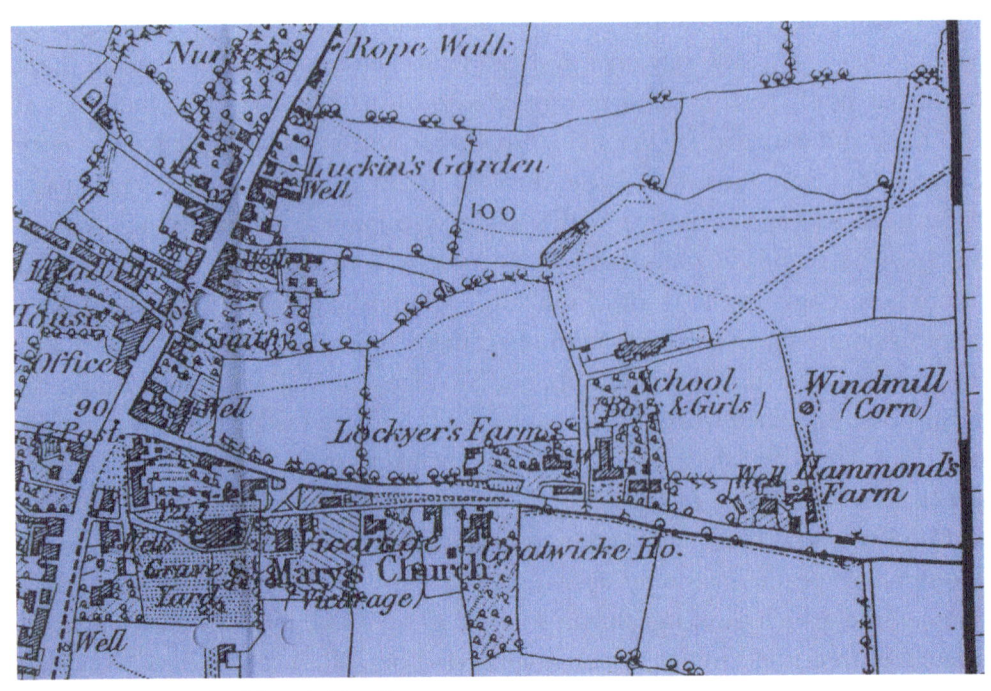

Map showing main buildings in East Street

Cocksbrook alias Hammonds north of East Street

1327/32

The earliest records of the area to the north east of Billingshurst, according to the documentation of John Hurd, suggest that one Johne de Kockesbroke or Cokkesbrouk gave his name to a piece of land subsequently known as Cockbrookes. [It is possible, of course, that Johne derived his name from his dwelling near a small stream called Cock's or Couk's brook!] The Lay Subsidy Roll of 1327 records the existence of Bellingesherst, with 41 inhabitants paying taxes.

Coxbrook, East and North of East Street, was a small part of the Hundred of West Easwrith, which comprised 12 parishes.

A lady called Alice Dawkes held 1 ½ virgates and a tenement called Crouchers. The parcel of land called Daux derives from her name and there was another area nearby called Broomfields. Coxbrook was larger that these other two combined.

There were 10 tithings in the Half-hundred of Easwrith. John Couk is one of those listed for the tithing of Billyngeshurste, amongst others like Somere, Gilmyn and Okhurst, names still extant in local place names.

1400AD

In the same year, when Geoffrey Chaucer died, William Dakons was paying 9s, 5d for Croucheslond and 5 shillings for Cookesbrouke.

1485

Tudor Times

1530

With the accession of King Henry VII in 1485, Tudor monarchs brought peace and prosperity to England.

It is likely that Hammonds, as it was later called, was coterminous with Cockesbrook to the north of the present A272 described as one ferlyng. However it appears to cover about 60 acres. In the early16th century Crouchers and Cockesbrook, together making 90 acres, constituting a parcel of the Manor of Pynckhurst, was held by John Gryndfyld [Greenfield?] of Daks [Daux]. One Thomas Greenfield also of Daux died in 1578.

Hammonds House

Hammonds is not one of the oldest houses in the village. The aptly-named Old House at Adversane dates from 1470 and the farmhouse called Great Daux, with its black and white elevation and half-hipped roof of Horsham stone and a notable crown post, near the railway station, was also first built in the 15th century. [William Evershed, who founded the Unitarian Church, lived there as did his family for many generations. Dr. Arthur Evershed, born there in 1836 was a celebrated artist. His son Thomas, with Jane his wife and son John succeeded him].

Great Daux, 15th Century house

1564

Shakespeare was born

1559-1565

Church Porch

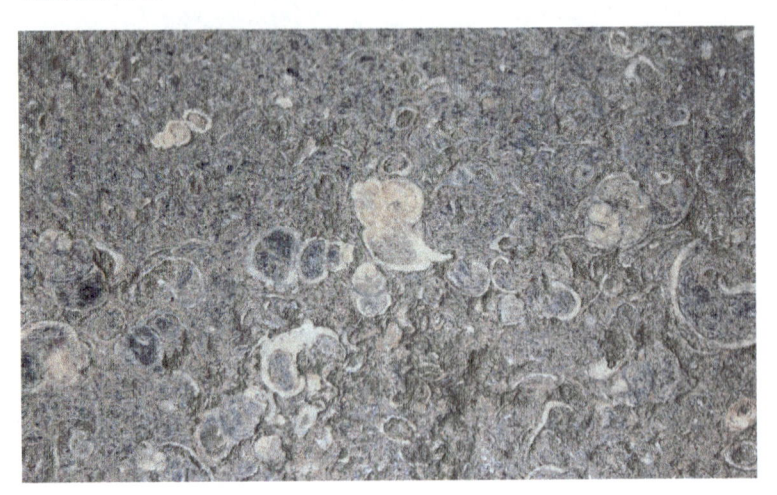

Winklestone on the porch floor

St. Mary's Church had its entry porch of brick and timber added in 1559, with slabs of winklestone or Sussex marble as flooring.

In 1565 Francis Garton, Gentleman, of Billingshurst took on a lease by copyhold for £140 for 10,000 years from Henry, Earl of Arundel of both Croochers, [tenement, yardland and one virgate] and Cockbrookes. To this he added a half virgate called Chesemans. William Garton had been the bailiff of the Manor of Bassett's Fee in 1553.

1557

Croochers and Cockbrookes were assigned to Richard West, Yeoman

1581

In 1581 a lease passed to John Apsley and William Lee, yeoman for all three parcels

1591

Richard West, son Richard, wife Margery all die. The Inventory value of his property was £206. 3s

1600-1618

In these years one Isaac Bungar was active in both Wisborough Green and Billingshurst, buying up woodlands to make window glass, an industry that demanded copious amounts of coppiced timber for fuel. The industry had prospered in Elizabethan times at Chiddingfold and Kirdford largely because of skilled French Huguenot immigrants. By 1612 in Staffordshire coal became the preferred fuel and in 1615 the use of wood was outlawed by Royal Proclamation and Bungar was obliged to shut down his wood-fired furnace. Few traces of this industry remain in Billingshurst.

1605

In 1603 the Elizabethan Poor Law was enacted to deal with the perceived threat of rogues, vagabonds and the welfare of the destitute. About 1605 the Billingshurst churchwardens funded '4 little rooms for the poor of the parishe' fronting East St. in Gorefield, part of Cocksbrook, at a cost of £4-10s-2d. These almshouses cost the parish £1-1s-10d for mending and thatching in 1641 and were on record to 1661. They may have constituted the earlier workhouse accommodation, predating the 'Old Workhouse'.

James I and the Stuarts

1605

The Gunpowder Plot was thwarted. Bonfire Night was celebrated in Billingshurst for many years. The tradition has recently been revived.

1610

We learn that in 1610 William Lee still held three parcels of land. He alienated 20 acres to Edward Grinfeild. Both were ordered to do fealty' [take an oath of fidelity of the vassal to the lord].

1612

In 1612 John Fuste of Itchingfield left Lockyers Farm, south of East Street, to his grandson John Shelley. It later passed to John Charman, whose name 'Charmans' is also used for Lockyers.

1630

Anthony Haman [? Hammond] paid Church Tax for Coxbrok. He had married Susan Lee in 1603 and presumably acquired title to the property. The earliest parish register for the village dates from 1630.

1639

Baron Edward Apsley, Knight, had a tenement nearby called Hilland with Thomas Henshaw acting as steward. Anthony Hammond was noted as being at Cocksbrook, with Lee at the other two parcels.

It is reasonable to suppose that this prosperous period in the 17th century would have been the time when Anthony Haman and his Lee relatives had a tenement erected, probably with adjacent barns, cowsheds and similar buildings. However the grade II listing for Hammonds, as now established, describes it as an 18th century building – 'Two windows, Painted brick, Modillion eaves cornice, Half-hipped roof of Horsham slabs, Trellised wooden porch with door of 6 fielded panels'. It has a 'dentil course' under the eaves, a line of bricks arranged to look like teeth. The present restored adjacent barn with tarred weather-boarding probably dates from the 17th century.

Hammonds House shows two clear stages of construction. The frontage, under the Horsham stone roof, is the original part, though it is possible that an even earlier building stood on the same site. There may well have been an outshot attachment on the rear north side. The central inglenook fireplace suggests an early date. The chimney stack is an echo of Elizabethan structures and by serving hearths on two storeys with attic rooms above, it indicates a middle 17th century date. One might speculate that the original timber-framed house on three storeys, with wattle and daub walls, both inside and out was built about 1650 and then had major revisions at 100 year intervals in 1750 or so and again in 1852.

The first alterations to Anthony Hamman's place would have entailed covering the original frontage with a brick skin and formalising the windows and porch after the fashion of the 18th century. Extra rooms were probably on the rear. At this point the west elevation may have been given its elaborate tile hanging as a defence against the rain of the prevailing wind and to enhance its appearance from the road. John Streeter would have had the necessary wealth at a time of prosperity in farming. By the same token when William Sprinks was prospering as a miller and farmer about 1850, landowner and tenant might well have undertaken the major conversion to a double roofed property when the mill and adjacent farm buildings were also erected.

1. Inglenook fireplace at Hammonds

2. Hidden date recording Victorian Extension

Inventories of goods and chattels left by Richard and Anthony Hammond, Anthony Haman's heirs, imply that the original house then had a central Hall with a table and seven 'joind stools' and four chairs. It had a Chamber or main bedroom above furnished with two feather beds and bolsters, 'bedstedles' a table and chests. Also on the ground floor was a Buttery or drink store and pantry with barrels, firkins and kilderkins (16 gallon storage casks). In the buttery loft chamber were kept a bed, a dozen pairs of sheets, two dozen odd napkins and half a dozen table cloths and 'pillow coats'. There was also a Milk Room with ten 'milk trees' [probably trays, pans used to settle milk ready for skimming off the cream], two cheese presses, a dozen 'truggs'. Again it had a lodging chamber above. This milk room was an indoor dairy where butter was made and cheese from skim milk.

There is no mention of third floor attic rooms, possibly because they had no possessions in them, and were used as servants' dormitories. On the ground floor was a Kitchen, with a table and forms, well endowed with twenty-four pieces of pewter, brass kettles and 'posnets' (3 legged pots) and iron vessels, a mortar, spoons, a shredding knife, candle sticks, salts, bellows, chamber pots, a warming pan, 'buckits', colander, basting ladle, a cleaver, spits and smoothing irons and a little 'foulling peece'. The Outlet Room or brew house was, perhaps, a utility space where there was a 'bucking tub' used for boiling clothes, a copper and mash tub where malt was mixed with hot water to form wort for brewing beer, and 'other lumber'.

1. Buttery vats

2. Butter churns

3. Cheese-making equipment

4. Cooking devices all as shown at Singleton Museum.

Elsewhere was the Malthouse, possibly in the High Street, where the malt was valued at £20 with the wire screen and 20 quarters of barley. In addition there was malting equipment –a vat, bushel and peck measures, 'linen and woollen wheells', an oast haire (haircloth used for drying hops) sacks etc. There was an outside barn with £7 of wheat grain and hay. They had one 'best horse' and a mill powered by a 'nagg' moving in a circle, 7 'smal pigs and 3 hoggs', 3 cows and one calf. The animals were valued at between £1 and £2 each. Anthony had bees and a 'beehouse' valued at £1.10s. There was a dung cart, a harrow and other 'husbandry tackling', tools, wood, 'faggats', a ladder and 'other lumber'.

A man's wealth, if he was not a landowner, rested in his possessions and the copper, silver and gold in his purse. It is easy to forget that there were then no branch banks or building societies in Billingshurst to care for the money of ordinary people in bank accounts, no chequebooks, no banknotes or safe facilities until the 20th century, and no Post Office offering 'postal orders' until the 19th. Goods and services changed hands for coins. Servants and wholesalers were paid in cash. [A private company had invented 'money orders' in 1792 and 'Postal Orders' descended from them. Very wealthy people might use City or provincial banks such as at Horsham who issued their own local notes, or make use of 'Bills of Exchange' to transfer money. The first coloured Bank of England banknotes were issued in 1927. £1 and 10s notes on white paper began during WW I to save gold and silver.] Farmers and traders, millers and maltsters would necessarily have been careful keepers of their business accounts, with a safe place to store their money, and reliant on lawyers to deal with their property rights and those of their heirs.

When Richard died his apparel and purse were valued at £31 and Anthony's at £8. Business was done in cash and by barter. Richard had money for malt owing to him 'on book' for £9-15s-4d when he died. A man could will to his heirs the property he owned, the real estate he had legal title to and the cash he had stored in his keeping. He might be able to borrow from or owe money to others, with or without interest, against properly accountable legal documents, but the concept of a loan from a branch bank to buy or sustain property was quite foreign to country people. Our modern practice of getting a mortgage from a local bank or other lender in order to purchase property dates only from the 1930s.

Barclays Bank was first housed near its present site in an old building after WW I. While this was being demolished in the 1960s it moved to the Parish Room beside the 10 Steps then back to the present premises. Lloyds Bank enjoys an unusual 1960s design and the Westminster Bank came in 1929.

A good deal of financial business in the 19th and early 20th centuries would have been conducted through the Friendly Societies that acted as savings banks and provided mutual insurance against ill health and other calamities. Charitable semi-Masonic bodies met and offered a venue for local traders to make deals. The Rhodes family for example were members of the Royal Antediluvian Order of Buffaloes which met regularly at the King's Arms.

Malting was made easier in the High Street where there was a handy stream, stone slabs to cool the barley to allow it to germinate and cordwood for the kiln. The process was for grain to be tipped into a shallow pit to soak and swell. It was then drained and transferred to a 'couch', lying about a foot deep and frequently turned, creating heat and beginning to germinate. In a couple of days or so it was spread out on a growing floor until roots began to appear. The stem had swelled up and just before it burst out of the husk it was left to dry. It was gradually moved to the kiln for three or four days, separated from the fire by a wire screen. Next it was sieved to remove the shoots and stored for some months to develop flavour. Most work was done in winter when farm workers were free to help. Malt Tax was exacted from 1697, then 6d a bushel, rising to 4s-6d by 1804, with complex rules of production to safeguard the interests of the taxman.

At the rear of the original Hammonds building is a substantial addition extending along the length of the front with its own roof, built of stone as an extension, probably in 1852. It is quite possible that previous extensions on the back of the house were removed to make way for the Victorian addition.

East elevation of Hammonds showing the stone-built extension

West elevation showing decorative tile hanging

1640

By the will of Anthony Hammon, Yeoman, he makes 10 shilling bequests to the poor of Billingshurst, to his wife Susan, and his eldest son (also named Anthony). He also inherits Gilmans which his father had bought from John and William Penfold in 1632. Another son gets a featherbed, once his mother's at his house in Gaystreet, Chiltington. The third son, Richard, gets £5 when aged 21, and Coxbrook when Susan dies, plus a furnace from Anthony's house in Billingshurst. The fourth son Isacke also gets £5 at age 21 and the Gaystreet furnace. This son married Joan Nye in 1642. (He died in 1701). His daughter Anna got £50 at 21 or on marriage to Edmond Stringer, Susan similarly or on marriage to John Crutchlow, and his Godchildren a shilling each on request. A small bequest was often made in wills as proof that a person had not been unintentionally overlooked.

1642

Richard Hammond was duly noted as the holder of Cocksbrooke in the Manor of Pinkhurst in 1642.

1649

Civil war. Charles I beheaded. The Republican Interlude

1649

William Greenfield, the elder, master butcher, willed Duckmore, Catshill and Lockiers, Hyle and Heathfeild to relatives. This is a considerable landholding East of Billingshurst. Lockyers is the farm south of East St and east of St Mary's Church, now Gratwicke Close. Duckmore lies north-east of Coxbrook. The Greenfields, who also occupied Summers, must have been very wealthy and influential citizens of Billingshurst.

1660

Restoration of the Monarch, Charles II, and the Church of England

Another prominent Sussex family, the Gratwicks, held Ifold Farm for 50 years which was part of the Billingshurst Manor of Bassetts Fee.

1665

In 1665 Richard Hammond and Matthew Weston were Churchwardens. They contributed to a fund for distressed Ancient Protestants, the Waldenses, who were being persecuted under the Duke of Savoy. There is clearly still a residual sympathy for Low Church values in the parish. The following year was that of the great fire of London.

1667

Richard was again elected Churchwarden along with Maurice Greenfield of Southhouse.

1675

Eight years later Richard was still at Cockesbrook. Thomas Stirt was at Dawks and Sigismund Stidolph of Headly at Broomfields.

1680

Richard Hammond, maulter [maltster], died in 1680. The inventory value of his property in his will was £98 -1s-11d. His eldest daughter Susan, born 1647, who was married to John Booker 1677, yeoman, of Rudgwick, gets 10s and a chest in the hall marked SH; his daughter Ann, married to R. Denn of W Chiltington, gets 10s; the youngest daughter, Rachel, gets £20. His son, Anthony is the executor and heir to the estate. Messrs. Pilfold and Ryde of Horsham are 'overseers'.

1682

In this year the last trial for witchcraft took place at Horsham. Only four out of eighteen witches tried in Sussex were found guilty and only Margaret Cooper of Kirdford was hanged, also at Horsham.

Isaac Hammond, Richard's brother, became Churchwarden in 1682. He paid £6.5s.6d to the Collectors.

Anthony Hammond, maulter and yeoman, died on the 9th January 1682 enjoying his property for only two years. His father, Richard, lived a long life compared to his son. The inventory of his goods and chattels valued them at £120.

By Anthony's will his grandchildren Jane and Reenald, (Ann and Denn's children), get £3 each, Susan's two children, John and Susan, £3 apiece, sister Rachel £80 from Billingshurst land and tenements and she shares the household goods with her sister Susan. Susan is the sole executrix. She inherits the freehold lands and tenements in Billingshurst, but if she does not pay Rachel her £80, then Rachel gets them! Susan's son-in-law, John Booker, and his heirs are to succeed on Susan's death.

1685

In 1685 The Manor of Pinkhurst reported the seizure of a cow from Anthony and Richard Hammond; both now deceased, in order to secure debts of 30s and 40s respectively. The malting business for the Hammonds seems to be faltering at the end of the 17th century.

1714

18th Century – the Georgian Era

1725

The old Vicarage was built in East St. Queen Ann was dead; the last of the Stuarts had gone.

At that time an expensive substantial stone-built dwelling called Tower's (or Towse?) House was erected east of the Almshouses. A will of Mary Champion of Frimley leaves her Billingshurst properties mainly to the Bartholomew family, with provision of £50 to buy Tower's, 'for the use of poor labouring men'. Dated ?? 1725. So began the 'Old Workhouse', originally a large T-shaped building.

1. The Old Workhouse original

2. Today

1731

In 1731 15 people are listed as taken in to the workhouse. Phillip Greenfield, possibly in charge, was paid for repairs to the workhouse and adjacent 'Clarks House'.

1738

In 1738 John Booker held the lease of Cocksbrook, '1d heriot, relief and services'. But in the same year, John Streater pays Poor Tax of £3. 15. 2d for Little Eaton and Coxbrook, indicating an imminent change of ownership. The fortunes of the heirs of the Hammonds were doubtless in decline and those of the Streeters in the ascendant. It was at this time that a host of special 'rates' for a wide variety of good causes were consolidated by Act of Parliament into a single Poor Tax.

Billingshurst's Heritage

1760-1840

Thomas Gratwick paid Poor Tax on a house in Lockyers south of East St. He died in 1766 aged 86. The house, buildings and yard together with six fields and meadows and a small shaw or wood were subsequently occupied by Henry Charman, William Smart, George Alwyn, Arthur Greenfield, Elizabeth Puttock and Mary Hughes, James Fuller, Phillip Puttock, a journeyman miller and nurseryman and Richard Hughes, a carpenter. This takes the story of Lockyers to 1840 or so. The Ordnance survey map of 1877 misleadingly places the name Lockyers on the north side of East Street.

The Unitarian Church

1754

'The Preacher', William Evershed, and Wm. Turner, a farmer of Newbridge, raised the Baptist Church off the High Street, then known as South Street. Besides Carters, Kensetts, Turners and Trowers there are 126 Eversheds lying buried in the graveyard. Ever since the Restoration of the monarch Charles II nonconformists had met in farm houses in the Horsham district. Matthew Caffyn, the 'Battle-axe of Sussex' practised Adult Baptism, and was imprisoned five times for heretical preaching before the Toleration Act of 1689. Though he died in 1714 the Horsham General Baptist Chapel began in 1721. The Billingshurst members wanted their own place. Evershed and Turner paid three guineas for the site off

South Street, transferring it to ten trustees for 1000 years. Initially it ran jointly with Horsham with the same Elders and rules, but a theological dispute about the 'laying on of hands' led, in 1818 to a parting of the ways and the appointment of a Billingshurst Minister. The Vestry was enlarged in 1886. It was used as a Library and a Sunday school, teaching the three Rs as well as piety. The clock, by Inkpen of Horsham is dated 1756. Pevsner praises the building, 'like a demure Georgian cottage on a knoll in a surprisingly big churchyard'. The Church was later renamed 'The Free Christian Church' and then 'The Unitarian Church'.

1766

In 1766 two men fell to their deaths while reshingling St. Mary's Church spire.

1767

Thomas Pacey, whose father was Thomas Pacy who died in 1715, a Yeoman, comes into the action, when it is reported in the records of the Manor of Pinkhurst that he had sold the freehold of the place called Hammonds and Cocksbrook to William Streater, miller of Billingshurst. Presumably he had bought it from John Booker about 1738.

Summers Place today

The area known as Summers on the road from Billingshurst to Five Oaks was owned in the mid 14th century by Richard Somer, on land presented to the Norman Earl Roger de Someri over a century earlier. Roger held two Knights

Fees in Billingshurst and Kirdford, the gift of Edward I. In 1372 Richard made a purchase of land from William Newbrigge [Newbridge]. Summers was effectively owned and occupied by the Greenfields from about 1484 to 1690. It was part of the Manor of Bassett's Fee.

Thomas Bettesworth of London, a Merchant, who died in 1795 and is commemorated in the parish church, built a large and handsome Georgian mansion-house about 1790 which was demolished some eighty years later. It was rebuilt in 1880, designed by an amateur architect, John Norton, for Robert Goff who let the property to F.D. Leyland Esq. To improve his view Old Pratts, opposite the Drive, was demolished and two late Victorian cottages built nearer the village to replace it. They are now used as offices. The New Road, as we now call it, was a rerouting of the old road which ran much closer to the mansion. Summers Place was subsequently sold to Henry Carnsew and then to Major Pratt. Col. Greenwell owned it from 1920 to 1945 when it became the Convent and School of The Sisters of the Immaculate Heart of St. Mary. In its heyday there were 40 boarders there and 120 day pupils. It closed in 1984 and until 2005 was Sotheby's provincial fine art auction house. This area is often spelt Somers in the records as in the tithing of Somere.

The boundaries of the Manor of Pinkhurst were defined [1766 to 1827] when the 'bounds were trodden': "W up Catshill to boundary (No.17) thence over the hedge into Cocksbrook and along the E side of Cocksbrook, leaving Duckmore on the right to (18) then up the N side of Cocksbrook to (19) by a stile, thence over the hedge and under the W hedges & then under the N hedge to (20) thence over into and under the N hedge of the Hammonds and Workhouse Garden to (21) in the Gore Fields hedge, thence round the Gore Fields and Old Platt, into a garden to (22) thence under the N side of said garden between Miss Pannells house in Billingshurst Street & Duckmore House in the Street held by the Manor of Bassetts Fee to boundary (1)".

1777

In the Report of a National Commission on Workhouses there are 45 places available in the Billingshurst institution.

1779

William Streater Senior was paying Poor Tax for Hammonds and Coxbrook in 1779.

1782

He paid Land Tax too. He also owned Taintlands and part of Gingers (Jengers) occupied by his son, also named William.

1795

William Streater Senior died in 1795.

By his will, he bestowed the Windmill and granary on Taintland and Gingers Farm to his Grandson William "with full and free liberty at any time with carts wagons and horses to and from the windmill". His son John got £700 from the estate, grandsons James and John [other children of his son, also named William] got £100 each at age 21 & 'and I hereby charge the windmill and the granary with the same.' His wife Elizabeth was to have £15 a year paid by his son William. [Messrs. Poltock and Holden were named as Trustees] - present messuage and tenement 'where I now live, garden, orchard farm barn lands etc. known as Hammonds and Coxbrook and wife Elizabeth the use of the messuage for life – to sell the same. His son William got Taintlands and Gingers (£15 payable to mother for life –'sans waste'). After his death the Trustees were to sell the property and invest the money towards the upbringing of his grandsons William, James and John.

Meantime in the wider world at a place called Speenhamland magistrates met and instituted a system whereby farm workers' wages were fixed, but when the price of bread rose above a critical figure they were to be paid a 'dole' from the Poor Rate. It was a disaster for all but the richer landowners. It kept wages so low that it pauperised honest workmen and weighed heavily on those who had to pay the Rate. The effect was clearly evident in Billingshurst

Billingshurst's Heritage

The Six Bells, formerly the farm house called Taintland

William Streater's will is the first real evidence of the house and property we now call Hammonds though it must have been built much earlier.

Taintland was a 16th century half-timbered farmhouse. It is now a pub in the High Street, the only house in Billingshurst with a continuous overhang or jetty along the whole first floor. It became a beer house in Victorian times. It was named Six Bells when St. Mary's Church belfry gained two more bells than the original six in 1897 to celebrate Queen Victoria's Diamond Jubilee. Bell Cottage is a 17th century building, originally thatched, which stands at the rear.

The old mill burnt down on Guy Fawkes Day, 1852. It is now only recorded by Mill Lane and Mill Way.

A hundred yards west of Hammonds House is Vine Cottage, built in the 18th century. About 1790 a brewer at the malting in the High Street lived there and in 1858 Thomas Baker, the 'Relieving Officer'. A Mr. Wm. Lorenzo Flight sold it in 1860 to the Voice family who lived there till 1919. Edward Voice who died in 1894 was a stone mason, plumber and painter. Between the world wars it was owned by seven different people, mainly maiden ladies. Miss Goddard and Miss Macintosh sold it, in 1953, to Miss Elder who sold it in turn to Alistair Morris, Chartered Surveyor.

Just west of the old workhouse is the 16th century or earlier Gore Farm house, one of the few Billingshurst buildings praised by Pevsner: 'half-timber frame, tile-hung front with a half-hipped gable at the w end: very pretty'. This judgement is despite the fact that the frontage is obscured by another building. Gore Farm is a late mediaeval hall house, though a floor and upper storey have been added, and it was extended in the 16th century, the addition now in separate ownership. The building was used as a tannery in the 17th century. At the time of this writing it is offered for sale for £450,000.

1. Vine Cottage, west of Hammonds

2. Gore Farm house.

3. Bell Cottage

4. Horsham Stone roofing

1798

In 1798 Denyer and Carter, Churchwardens, and Turner and Greenfield, Overseers of the Poor, signed Articles of Agreement for Moses Chantler, a tenant farmer at Wooddale, to provide for the poor of the parish at a cost of £1000.

The 19th Century

1801

The 1801 Poor Tax evaluation on William Streater shows him due to pay on Taintland and Gingers (41 ½ acres) with a house and Duckmore (54 ½ acres) with houses. This constitutes a considerable farmland holding. The widow of Wm. Streater Sr. and John Johnson were also taxed for part of Hammonds House. Sir Abraham Hume owned Brookfields, and Miss Leagatt Great Daux, both of which were occupied by Wm. Evershed. Lady Bartholomew owned Summers where Mr. Jeal lived.

1804

The Manor of Pinkhurst reported that Hammonds/Cocksbrook was held freely by William Streater, miller, a bankrupt. His business was clearly in trouble as was Europe, with the Napoleonic war well under way.

The Reverent P. Evershed successfully challenged the cruel 'sport' of cock throwing and cock fighting by pinning a critical poem on his church door. Weighted sticks called 'libbets' were hurled at tethered cocks. People used to come from miles around on Shrove Tuesday to see this gruesome spectacle.

1805

There was victory and tragedy. Nelson died at the Battle of Trafalgar in 1805.

1806

The Hammonds property, freehold land and tenement, was alienated by the assignees, that is to say, unpaid creditors, to John Streeter, William's brother, a farmer. He may well have been bankrupt too.

William managed to father a bastard son, baptised Henry Roberson, by Charlotte Robinson at the Common Workhouse in East Street. The miller and Charlotte were to appear before the magistrates at the Half Moon, Petworth.

The family history of the Streaters suggests rich source material for an historical novel along the lines of Hardy's 'Mayor of Casterbridge' with its rags to riches theme and subsequent poverty and disgrace.

1809

John Streater was still paying rent and Land Tax in 1809.

1811

Charlotte, the mother of Wm Streeter's child, was baptised in 1789, married in 1811 and died 1842.

1812

Charles Dickens was born.

1814

John was paid 4d for carting stone from Stammerham, now the site of Christ's Hospital, for the belfry at the Parish Church just before the battle of Waterloo.

'Stammerham' actually means 'dwelling near a stone quarry'. Horsham stone is a thin, fine grained, calcareous sandstone laid down about 120 million years ago in the Cretaceous age of the dinosaurs, occurring quite close to the surface in an arc South and West of Horsham. Extensive old pit workings are evident at Cowfold. The Romans valued its tough properties in their building of Stane Street (= Stone from the Norse 'steinn') Street which runs through Billingshurst and subsequent builders appreciated the way it splits easily along the bedding planes for use as roofing slabs and walling blocks. We don't know what the Romano-Brits called it.

The Saxon term is first recorded in 1270 as 'Stanstret'.

Another valuable rock also occurs in the Lower Weald Clay. This is 'Sussex Marble', a compressed limestone composed of fossilised winkle-like gastropods (molluscs), which can be highly polished for fonts, tombs, mantelpieces, columns and fireplaces, and used for floor slabs as they were at St. Mary's Church. When the Billingshurst by-pass was built seams of the marble were exposed. It has been found at Stonepits in Marringdean Road. It is likely that it might be found under Hammonds as beds excavated at Coolham as recently as 1903 run West towards Billingshurst. The stone was laid down 125 million years ago. Though decorative it is not a rock suitable for building. Further south the building stone found in the Upper Greensand was deposited 110 million years back, and the chalk which contained flints for building and sharp tools is 100 million years of age. Eventually the Wealden clay of the Billingshurst area finally yielded a dividend with the development of local brick and tile making required for the vernacular architecture in the later Victorian expansion. At Wildens along from East Street is the site of a great brickyard with four kilns mapped in 1879. Here clay flower pots and tiles were made. There was also a brick field in Station Road, behind the first three houses in Silver Lane, another at the end of what is now Brookers Road and the Station Brickyard on the site of the current Gilmans Industrial Estate.

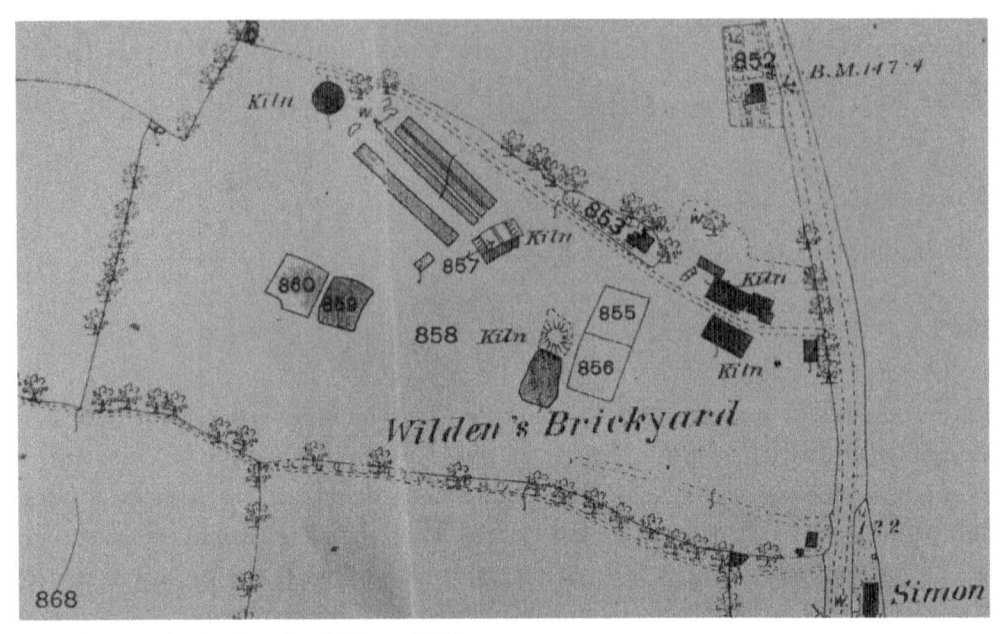

Map showing the Brickyard and kilns at Wildens

1816

The Wey and Arun Canal opened, linking London to Portsmouth. In 1817 27 tons of goods were moved from Arundel and a similar amount to London and a week later a similar cargo came back. For half a century it boosted local trade but with the competition of the railway it had become uneconomic and closed in 1863.

1817-1830

There was trouble at the Workhouse in 1817 when Renolds Totham, the Governor, was in debt and obliged to surrender his effects to his creditors. The Vestry advertised for a 'Man [without family] who understands the sack rope and woollen manufactory to superintend the poor house as Governor thereof' – no doubt to make simple work for the inmates- ; 'also for persons to visit twice a week with power to make or alter regulations etc.' In 1830 Simon Johnson, and wife, were appointed to care for the paupers, and later to superintend the road workers.

1822

John Streater and James Trower are now paying Land Tax in 1822.

1823

Streater was paying Poor Tax just for Hammonds House, while James Trower paid for Great and Little Rowfold, part of Priors, Hoile, Little Daux, and Hammonds. This is the first mention of the Trower family who figure significantly in later years.

1. The East Mill

2. The young tree in the 70's

3. Recent

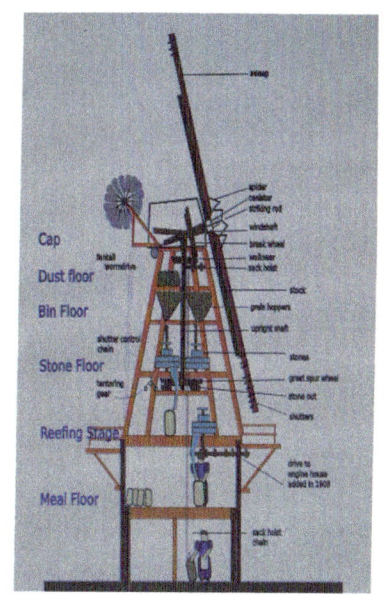

4. a diagram showing typical construction

1825

By the evidence from inscription over the door, "JS 1825" now lost, the East Windmill was built in 1825 by John Streeter with Richard Chennell as the miller. The walls of the mill would have been tarred to resist damp affecting the flour and to protect the walling stones from the weather. It was a smock mill raised on an octagonal stone base with an upper storey faced with horizontal wooden planks and a revolving cap designed to turn into the wind and carrying four large 'sweeps' or sails. The erection of a second mill in Billingshurst reflects the growing demand and profitability of cereals in early 19th century England.

1827

Richard Chennell is now paying Poor Tax for his house, Hammons Land and the Windmill and Mrs. Evershed for Hammons House.

1830

The King's Arms, ancient coaching inn.

William Cobbett mentions The King's Arms in his 'Rural Rides'. He breakfasted well there. However farm workers were starving. They could not afford the high price of wheat caused by the demands and blockades of the Napoleonic Wars.

(1803-1815). 1000 men assembled in Horsham, and compelled the magistrates to agree a wage of half a crown a day. The County Gaol at Horsham was swiftly filled with demonstrators! Fearing an attack on the gaol the Government moved in regiments of Life and Foot Guards. It became known as the 'Mobbing Winter'. Throughout England farm workers threatened magistrates, Poor Law guardians and rich tenant farmers by anonymous letters, signed 'Captain Swing' demanding better wages, relief from Poor Tax, an end to tithes and the destruction of new threshing machines, seen as a threat to employment. The name 'Swing Riots' was given to the insurrection allegedly from the name of the hinge on a threshing flail. Cobbett defended the rural labourers and was tried for sedition for his pains. He was acquitted.

One consequence of the riots was the Great Reform Act of 1832, and another the setting up of Workhouses in 1834 to give shelter to the indigent. This reform was deemed necessary because of the burden of poor rates. They had risen from £2m in 1785 to £10m in 1818. However the rioters were initially brutally suppressed, 19 being hanged, 644 imprisoned and 481 transported to Australia. The early Victorian recipe for dealing with the ever-threatening danger of insurrection by the underclass, the unpriviliged majority of Disraeli's 'Two Nations', was a cunning mixture of the velvet glove, philanthropy with charity and social and political reform, and the mailed fist, punishment by imprisonment, transportation and execution. The workhouses were designed to deter any shiftlessness or welfare-scrounging by offering only miserable regimes, by separating families, and by providing only cheap food and hard labour.

1831/41

Billingshurst is recorded as having 1540 inhabitants. Corn was bought and sold once a fortnight at the Kings Arms on Tuesday evenings. The 'Comet' coach offered a daily service to London and Bognor.[Pigot's Directory].Fish was brought to the village from Worthing in carts drawn by four or five dogs.

1832

John Streater was still paying Land Tax but Richard Chennell and William Bridger were now the occupants of Hammonds.

1837

Queen Victoria was crowned

The 1841 Tithe Apportionment states that Phillip Puttock and wife Ann, their son Edwin and wife, a gardener and two young grandchildren lived at Lockyers house, and so did Richard and Mary Hughes and four children. However there is also listed Gratwick House and Garden, the responsibility of Richard Farhall, a Gentleman of Tillington, who seems to be the landlord of all Lockyers together with Woodhouse and Wilden's Land. He was affluent enough to have a vote in Horsham Polling District and perhaps facilitated the building of the great new house sometime in the 1830s. However the will of Arthur Greenfield suggests that Farhall was a trustee holding the property for the benefit of his sister Elizabeth Puttock, her good friend and housekeeper, Mary Hughes and Phillip, her illegitimate son. When they died the sale profits would revert to Arthur's nieces and nephews.

Gratwick House

1834 to 1848

The year 1834 saw a new Poor Law enacted in response to low wages and the heavy rate demands of the Speenhamland system. 'Outdoor relief' was abolished and the 'workhouse test' imposed on applicants for public alms. Parishes were grouped together and enjoined to form Unions or central workhouses. Life in the workhouse was intended to be made deliberately unattractive to deter the shiftless. The likes of Charles Dickens in *Oliver Twist* exposed the inhumanity of this cruel process which separated husband, wife and children. Philanthropic sentiment slowly improved matters and the new Unions, run by elective Boards of Guardians were efficient, if unpopular.

It was decided in 1834 to pay the poorhouse master in East Street so much a pauper, depending on the price of good wholesome flour made from brown wheat. In 1836 Mr. Johnson was allowed to occupy the kitchen and pantry and two little rooms above, with a surveyor appointed to direct the necessary work. In 1838 the workhouse tenants 'had greatly abused the premises by destroying the windows and palings'. The Overseers had them boarded up. By 1839 the poor house was let out to James Fuller, a butcher, for £2 for one year. In 1840 the Overseers gave all the resident families notice to quit and to threaten those in the 'parish cottages' (almshouses) that unless they paid their arrears of rent by 1st Feb distress warrants would be taken out against their goods and chattels. Fuller's tenancy was then extended for 6 years at £10 per annum, with a cashback allowance of £4 for repairs, and agreement to give up the 'upper long rope shop' after due notice. It was duly taken down and sold in lots by auction in 1841. Fuller owed a year's rent of £10 so the Parish Officers were instructed to recover the money and recover possession. In 1848 there were just two caretakers in the old workhouse – 'no occupants allowed'.

By the Marriage Act of 1836 non-conformist and catholic people in Billingshurst no longer had to be wed by a Church of England parson, but could be married by their own ministers.

Kings Head Inn

Pigot's Directory of 1840 tells us of some of the personalities prominent in Billingshurst in the first years of Victoria's reign. The Reverends Henry Beath and Josiah Chapman were clergy and the 'Gentry' included John Ireland, John Napper, Magistrate, and George W. Wood at Summers. It states that The Duke of Norfolk is Lord of the Manor and holds a Court triennially. [A mistake! The Duke was not Lord of the Manor]. C.P. Goring. Bart. was Patron of the Living of St. Mary's Church. Professional persons included Wm. Boarer, day school, Matthew Caffin, land and timber surveyor, Peter Evershed, surgeon, and Henry Turner, Registrar of Births and Deaths and surveyor

Keepers of inns were Fred Peskett at The Blacksmiths, Adversane, a 17th century beer house, George Puttock at the Kings Arms and James Aylward at the Kings Head.

Shopkeepers and traders included David Baker, watchmaker, Cornelius Carter, blacksmith at Adversane, Stephen Evershed, Vetinary Surgeon, Edward Harwood, bootmaker, Adversane, Peter Kensett, grocer, draper and agent of the County Fire Office, Stephen Knight, maltster, three Lakers, tailors, leather sellers and hairdressers, George Puttock, basket, measure, sieve and hoop maker, William Sprinks, miller at Hammonds, John Voice, boot and shoemaker and Luke Wadey, wheelwright.

Many of these names have echoed down the years and are still familiar in the neighbourhood.

1840

Tithe acreage was assessed for payment by John Streeter and Wm Sprinks as follows: Garden Field 1.3.16 acres, Mill Field and East Windmill 5.2.17 acres, Hammonds House, Gardens and buildings 0.1.32 acres – about 8 acres in all. This must have included what is now Mill Barn and Hammonds, including the Garden Field now under development as 'Windmill Close'.

The workhouse plot, over an acre and occupied by Richard Farhall, the Lockyers landlord, had a separate tithe apportionment to be paid by Phillip Hughes and the 'parish cottage' was occupied by Abraham and Lydia Langley. (1841)

1841

The census of 1841 reveals that William Sprinks, aged 34 was now the miller of the East Mill (since 1839). He also ran the other older village mill. He had three wives; the first was Ruth who died in 1857 and was buried in the Baptist Chapel;

in 1859, aged 50, he married a widow aged 47 – Sarah Seward; finally he married Ruth Older at St. Nicholas, Brighton in 1861. The second Ruth outlasted him by 6 years dying in 1891. William died 1885, and was buried at the Baptist Chapel. There were three children all by the first Ruth. William was named once again as the miller in Kelly's Directory in 1845.

1845

The children were William, b. 1830, Emily, b. 1834 who married Robert Bishopp in 1853, and Albert, b. 1838 who married Victoria Ann Worsfold, aged 20 and died 1880 aged 35. Albert Henry Sprinks died in 1887, aged 49. By 1874, according to the Sussex Directory, he was based at the Station Commercial Inn, licensed to let horses and a railway carrier. Mrs. Victoria Sprinks was still there in 1909. The Railway Hotel, as it was later named, sold beer brewed by Michell of Horsham. [Henry Michell (died 1874) was a wealthy local dignitary worth £40,000. He was a brewer, owner of pubs, brickmaker and investor in water and rail companies and friend of the Shelleys of Warnham. He left much of his wealth to his daughter Fanny who was married to Thomas Cowan who lived at Comptons Lea, Horsham for 20 years. Cowan became the most famous writer and 'Father of British Beekeeping'. Michell's son, also called Henry inherited the brewery business.] The present Railway Inn has a new facade.

1. The Old Railway Hotel

2. The present Railway Inn and listed Signal Box

William Sprinks had two live-in servants, Edward Wells, 25, journeyman miller, and Charles Fuller, 19, manservant.

1848

In 1848 William Sprinks was named as a Constable, together with Joseph Dale of Five Oaks, Hez. Miles, farmer of Soil Farm, Adversane, John Nicholson, farmer, James Trower, draper of Billingshurst, James Towse, farmer of Kingshall, David Baker, Billingshurst a watchmaker and William Evershed, farmer at Tedfold.

Wm. Sprinks, miller, is on record as signing a Vestry minute. This set of local worthies, no doubt, were representative of the leading personalities of the Billingshurst community who conducted parish business through the Vestry Meeting.

1848 is remembered as the 'Year of Revolutions'. In England there was alarm among the ruling establishment when 150,000 Chartists assembled in London to present a petition for an extended franchise. As a result 100,000 special constables were recruited nationwide.

The Officials of the Parish Vestry

The position of Constable is the oldest parish official title. It was established by the 12th century as an appointment and executive authority of the Manor Court to enforce law and order. Thomas Grenfeld, Constable of West Easwrith in 1622, dealt with repairs to the Hundred Pound at Billingshurst where straying animals were constrained. Special Constables were instituted by Charles II to counter public disorder in 1673.

From 1842 the recommendation for appointments of constables was formally transferred to the parish Vestry, who also paid the wages, subject only to the approval of the Magistrate. The Constable had powers of arrest and the duty of constraining felons in stocks or cage prior to appearing before the Magistrate. They were expected to report crimes, deal with rogues and vagabonds, supervise alehouses, drunkards, lewd persons and other trouble-makers and conduct the whipping of stray dogs and vagrants as occasion demanded. One duty was to apprehend the putative fathers of bastard children! Their responsibilities were summed up as 'keeping watch and ward'. These duties were shared with the Churchwardens and Overseers and individuals often assumed two or more of the titles. They supervised the pillory and the ducking stool wherever that practice occurred. These were grave responsibilities and no doubt were often more honoured in the breach than the observance when entrusted to such as Shakespeare's character, Dogberry, who reckoned the best way to deal with a thief was to let him 'steal out of your company'.

The County Police Act of 1839 allowed Counties to establish a full-time professional Force which became mandatory from 1856. The Western Sussex Force dates from 1851. Billingshurst was fortunate enough to have its own Police Office and resident Sergeant and two Constables living in two houses in Coombe Hill throughout much of the 20th century but, of recent years, policing has been exercised by mobile units and Community Support Officers. The Station was sold off as residential property.

Churchwardens were officially established as officers of the church in 1127 as the proper 'Guardians of the Church'. They shared responsibility for vagrants and the poor with the other appointees, the Overseers, and for keeping the accounts of all parish business. The Billingshurst Overseers had numerous duties. They levied rates, registered and administered apprenticeships for poor young people in the parish, controlled censuses, alehouses and fire engines. Though unlikely in Billingshurst they dealt with brothels and pawnbrokers. They also registered electors until 1918. The office was not finally abolished until 1925. The parish officials often raised additional funds for the church by the equivalent of the church fete or jumble sale. This was a 'Church Ale' where home-brew was drunk at the 'Church House', a forerunner of the Village Hall. The Billingshurst Parish Room once stood beside the Ten Steps off the High Street. Overseers of the Poor administered the Poor Law from 1601 to 1834. After that they were just rate collectors and assessors.

1. Hairdressers and 10 steps today

2. Crisp's Barber shop built 1895, and the Parish Room

Waywardens were appointed to keep the highways in order. Up to 1835 roads were mended by 'statute labour' whereby certain wealthier parishioners had to supply the Surveyor with draught animals, carts and labour when he needed them. With the abolition of statute labour repair became a charge on the parish rates. Farmers did continue to help and regular 'roadmen' were appointed, familiar figures until after WWII when they were replaced by mobile gangs. From 1903 when the speed limit rose to 20 m.p.h. and cars became available the steady process of tarring of roads began. The Vestry records tell of how, in 1846, the making of a new road was let by contract and how the Workhouse Governor also supervised road workers. Haywards, guardians of fences and enclosures, saw to the upkeep of hedgerows.

One other official was the Parish Clerk. He was paid a salary and was often the Assistant Overseer. In 1833 there is a record of a vestry decision to discharge the Billingshurst parish clerk and appoint another.

1798 to 1854

There was, by 1835, a Union Workhouse at Petworth, originally built at Hampers Green in 1820 for 112 inmates. The 'Union' was of several parishes so that the refuge was provided centrally and more economically than separately at each village. The Vestry, advised by the Board of Guardians, decided to dispose of the Billingshurst Parish workhouse property. In 1850 the building and ¾ acre garden was put up for sale by auction at the King's Arms with a reserve of £225 together with cottages at Five Oaks, East Lane and a plot in Marringdean Road, together valued at £78.

Thirty-two burials are listed in the Burial Register from the poorhouse and later workhouse between 1798 and 1854 and two more from the Union, a large workhouse, which served five parishes. Billingshurst had three representatives on the Board of Guardians. From 1870 Billingshurst sent its indigent parishioners to Horsham Union rather than Petworth.

It is a matter of some regret that the earlier village records are scanty regarding the names and lives of the working classes except for those paupers at the bottom of the social pyramid. The honest toilers, who did the physical work of the village, lived in impermanent dwellings, owned no real estate, paid no rates and had no gravestones. The record that survives, like the timber-framed houses they lived in, is chiefly remembered in the lives and doings of the yeomanry, traders and tenant farmers.

1850

The Manor of Pinkhurst records in 1850 that John Streeter 'late of Lancing' has died and his lands at Hammonds or Cocks Brook were seized 'whereon a windmill is erected'. He and his wife Mary had lived as paupers in East Lane? But John's daughter, Mary Ann had married Thomas Trower of Rowfold so all was not lost.

1851 Census – the year of the Great Exhibition in the Crystal Palace at Kensington

1851

William Sprinks was prospering as the miller and farmer of 52 acres at Shipley, employing 5 men. He had 4 servants – Wm Parker, a waggoner, aged 48, Thomas Voice, 16, general servant, Richard Tidy,16, apprentice miller, and Charity Johnson, servant. She married Isaac Dean.

Foice Champion, a pauper shoemaker, and his son Edward, a ploughboy, lived at the Old Workhouse.

Edward Wells, journeyman miller and Jane his wife were now at Lockyers. They had five children. Henry Bridgewater, an unmarried farm labourer, lived there too with a housekeeper, Sarah Briggs.

The Vicarage

1852

Major alterations took place at Hammonds House. It became double roofed with a stone extension along the rear, provided with handsome tile hanging to the west elevation. The wattle and daub frontage had probably already been given a new brick facade. The date of the rear addition was established when an inner timber was stripped to reveal the workman's carved date. Regeneration work in

Billingshurst in mid-century coincides with a prosperous period for farming and the first influx of wealthy people from elsewhere.

1858

The present Vicarage in East St was built in 1858, designed by S.S. Teulon, a famous London architect of the Victorian Gothic revival, who supervised hundreds of church and vicarage restorations.

The Railway Age

1859

The opening of the railway station in 1859 altered the way of life of the people of Billingshurst for good. Hitherto the village economy was based, fundamentally, on locally produced food and shelter. People milked their own cows, butchered their own pigs, malted their own barley for their own ale, quarried their own roof tiles, fired their own bricks, milled their own wheat, cut their own firewood, dug their own wells for water and made their own entertainment. The only imported items were sugar and spice and other ingredients that little girls are made of, and little luxuries they could afford to enjoy like tobacco, tea and coffee. Self-reliance and the necessity for neighbourly cooperation were essential. Tools to grow vegetables, wheels for the carts and horses to pull them, lime for the land and tithes and taxes to service the Vicar, the Workhouse School, the poor and the needy, all were locally forged, crafted or collected.

All movement was on foot or by horse. Certainly the old Roman Road had left Billingshurst the legacy of being a coach staging post. Carriers, using great wagons drawn by eight horses and guarded by a blunderbuss, operated regularly. The Comet coach, with twelve on top and four inside, left the Kings Head daily for London and the coast. But fares were so expensive that only people and light goods could be transported in or marketed at a distance. There were three turnpike gates between Billingshurst and Horsham alone. In 1820 a ride to London by coach cost £1-2s-0d, the equivalent of three week's wages for a farm worker! The Five Oaks Turnpike Trust netted £342 in the year 1845.

By the end of the 18th century those goods included tea, much of it smuggled, and sugar from the West Indies in sufficient quantities for them to become usual in the homes of cottagers. Formerly ale had been the main drink and honey the only sweetener.

Came the railway in 1858, came loads of coal and a gasworks and all the benefits of an industrialised society such as factory-made clothes and tools, imported bricks, groceries from all over the world, national newspapers and train tickets to London and the seaside. Local shopkeepers began to sell bread made from Canadian flour, Canterbury lamb and London beer and gin and cotton goods from home and abroad. Cotton often replaced the 'good old English' woollen cloth of earlier years, the stuff that in the late 18th century we were required by law to be buried in, on pain of a £5 fine for non-compliance. On the farms locally forged hand tools, sickles and scythes, flails and hoes, gave way to superior harrows and cultivators, and steam engines to power threshing machines and ploughs and stationary engines for workshops. Retail shops expanded and it became realisable to export local produce and indeed to multiply it by the founding of light industries like the making of flea powder and vacuum cleaners. For a time there was a cattle market just south of the station.

There was a downside of course. Although blacksmithing continued at Adversane and butchering and malting in the High Street, nevertheless a great many craftsmen on farms and in workshops were obliged to seek new work on building sites, in factories and in domestic service. A number emigrated to America, Canada and other Empire destinations. Workers in the coach and carrying trade at the Billingshurst Commercial Inns probably found employment from the railway and the Railway Inn was built. Harness and rope-makers, kiln workers, timber cutters, farm tool-makers, tailors, millers and ostlers gave place to the retail and motor trade, steam engineering, and the mending of bicycles.

Before bikes became popular in the 1890s ordinary Billingshurst folk had to walk everywhere. The bicycle transformed their lives in ways we scarcely appreciate. A horse would have cost a year's wages besides the provender and stabling costs. The commercial inns and transport businesses gained a temporary respite in the 20th century, with the advent of the internal combustion engine from cars and charabancs, only to lose trade again when the village was by-passed in 1994. Hill View garage, The Malaya, the Billingshurst Coach Station, Southern Counties and other outlets all flourished but finally disappeared to be replaced by dwelling houses and a Budgens supermarket. Many young people took off for work in London or the coastal towns.

1861

The 1861 census lists Hammonds, Mill House with William Sprinks still living as a widower with his son Albert and two different servants. These were Elizabeth Hutcheson, housekeeper, and Jane Aylward, dairymaid. Elizabeth Ewins, 13, was a visiting scholar. That same year William married Ruth at Brighton.

Moses and his wife Rhoda Wilson [nee Wadey], (a farm labourer) was in the Old Workhouse, with five children and a lodger, Edwin Puttock. Also listed are Mrs. Venn, whose husband had deserted, a seamstress aged 33 with four children, and Samuel and Barbara White, a brickmaker moulder with four children, one of whom, Ann, had a baby together with her brickmaker husband, William Richardson.

1862

By 1862 Mary Ann Trower, John Streeter's daughter, had died and her surviving husband, Thomas Trower, was reported by the Manor of Pinkhurst, to own the freehold, messuage and lands called Hammonds alias Cocksbrook.

Schools in Billingshurst

1. School timbers

2. Weald School

1865

In Shakespeare's time there was a keen regard for education. 'My brother Jacques he keeps at school and report speaks goldenly of his profit' [*As You Like It*]. In Billingshurst a religious Guild called The Brotherhood offered to pledge money to maintain a school. The road to Hell is paved with good intentions. Little tuition was available for poor scholars until the late 19th century.

The village school off School Lane in East St. was built in 1865, the gift of Henry Carnsew of Summers Place, and added to for infants in 1912. In 1972 it was used as a Church Centre and closed in 1973, though it was still utilised for some classes until 1991. It is now private residences.

Education that was available for a Billingshurst villager in the 18th century was in the type of child-minding institution known as a Dame School where a little reading and writing was taught by unqualified ladies. However lessons were provided even for pauper children in the Workhouse. The few moneyed local gentry would employ tutors and governesses and use the Grammar or Public Schools for their children. By reinvigorating Rugby School Dr Thomas Arnold had created an educational system for the landed gentry, the professional men and the new industrialists which served Britain and the Empire well. However it also served to weld together all the privileged classes into an exclusive old boy network which dominated the commanding heights in politics, the professions, the military and the judicature, to the detriment of the opportunities of a wider meritocracy. The legacy of that division of society remains with us.

During the 19th century elementary schooling for the less privileged slowly evolved, like most other social and welfare developments, under the leadership of the Vicar. There were a variety of private schoolrooms set up in the village for the lesser gentry such as The Crescent School in South Street. Wendy Lines tells of an Academy run by a Mr. Boorer, who may well have been aptly named, and of Miss Potter who ran a boarding school for girls. The Baptist Church had a school room and a library. More recently Mrs Murat ran St. Christopher's School on the corner of Daux Avenue and Audrey and Thomas Flynn had a boys' crammer prep school at Beke House in Marringdean Road. There was also the Convent School at Summers Place. Since 1961 at Ingfield Manor at Five Oaks, 'Scope', the charitable organisation which offers support for parents and conductive education for children with cerebral palsy, has enjoyed a national reputation for its service to disadvantaged youngsters.

The National Schools movement aimed to provide a school in every parish where orthodox Anglican doctrine could be assured and to establish Sunday Schools to reinforce the initiative. A Chartered School for Boys operated at the east end of the parish church. It was pulled down in 1866 when the church was 'restored'. Mr. Henry Wright was the Head. He and his son Ernest were Headmasters in the village for 68 years. 'Buzzy' Wright had a reputation for his enthusiastic use of the cane. He lived with his family at School House, and they helped run the classes. In those days all the teachers lived in the village. The village schoolmaster was modestly rewarded but, being literate, he could command esteem as Secretary of the Working Men's Club, counsellor and source of parental guidance.

'Lands he could measure, terms and tides presage,
And even, the story ran, that he could gauge.
While words of learned thought and thundering sound,
Amazed the gazing rustics ranged around.
And still they gazed and still the wonder grew,
That one small head could carry all he knew.
[Oliver Goldsmith 1770]

From 1833 government grants were available to charity schools subject to inspection by HMIs [Her Majesty's Inspectors]. The Revised Code of 1862 introduced the first 'National Curriculum', basically the three Rs for juniors and 'object lessons', an early version of 'show and tell', for Infants. Children were categorised into 'standards' or levels of achievement rather than by age, so that theoretically a slow learner, dismissed as a 'dunce', could stay in Standard I until he left school! Grants were only payable after the Inspector had certified acceptable results, punctuality and attendance. Thus the School Bell and the Attendance Register and keeping the Log Book were important tasks for the teachers who resented this system of 'Payment by results'. Billingshurst was at first a National

School under the aegis of the Diocese, but was taken over as a County School in 1910 when there were 240 children on roll.

In Victorian times demands for reform of the franchise and criticism of the poverty of ignorance by such as Charles Dickens and other evangelicals and philanthropists were prompting right-minded people everywhere to seek improvements to the literacy and numeracy of the work force. This was a special concern of Utilitarian thinkers who realised that expensive machinery and sophisticated engineering would be wasted without educated operatives. The culmination of this was the great Elementary Education Act of 1870 which set up School Boards to provide schooling everywhere, with qualified teachers, for children between 5 and 10. Attendance was not made compulsory though until 1880. The age of leaving was raised to 12 in 1880, to 14 in 1918, to 15 in 1944 and to 16 as recently as 1972.

Fees of a penny or two a week were still required from 1870 until 1891 when education became free. Payment by results was stopped in 1897. In 1902 School Boards were abolished and responsibility for education was vested in Local Education Authorities, which in West Sussex was the County Council. Characteristically the Parish Council took umbrage! A minute of 1905 reads: The Parish Council of Billingshurst view with great alarm and concern the enormous unnecessary and unreasonable increase in the cost of education since the local control has been vested in the County Council and ask the Council to give this matter their very serious consideration having due regard to the expenditure of the ratepayers' money.' Some of that expense will have been for the new mass-produced steel dip pens, with slit nibs required after 1870 to teach copperplate handwriting and for the cheaper powdered ink for the inkwells. Children at Adversane had the option of attending the school at North Heath.

At last there came some Secondary education when the school became 'all age'. Dr. Moreton was for many years the progressive and widely respected Headmaster (1937-51). Billingshurst School was the first in Sussex to provide hot dinners for the children in 1931 when Mr. Jeavons was the Headmaster. A dinner cost 3 old pence and 10% were free, served in a shed provided by the Beck sisters. A new Junior School and a separate Infants School were built at the entrance to Station Road in the early 1970s.

Cricket and football were played in the Bowling Alley and on the site of the present St. Gabriel's Catholic Church, with a Nissen hut as a changing room. Lent was the traditional marbles season for boys and skipping for girls. Good Friday was called 'Marble Day' or 'Long Rope Day'. Hoops made of iron, pop-guns made from elder wood, catapults and conker battles had their seasons.

A few clever children won 'scholarships', gaining places at Grammar Schools in

Horsham, Steyning or Midhurst. These 'all age' arrangements persisted until the Weald Secondary Modern School opened in 1957, taking in pupils at 11+ from many adjacent villages. Finally, in 1969 the Weald became Comprehensive and the Grammar Schools no longer recruited only selected pupils. Collyers School in Horsham became a Sixth Form College and the Girls' High School became a co-educational 11 to 16 comprehensive and was renamed Tanbridge House. The Weald School has been the subject of four major building extensions since its inception. It now constitutes an extensive campus with sophisticated modern facilities. It is the biggest employer in the district and is numbered among the best 10% of secondary schools in the country.

'Standards' persisted in primary schools until the 1940s. In 1879 a competent Standard VI pupil, ready to leave school, was expected to be able to: 'read with fluency and expression', write a short theme or letter with consideration for grammar, spelling and handwriting or write to dictation; to understand proportion, vulgar and decimal fractions; parse and analyse a short complex sentence; know the outlines of the geography of the world and of the history of England from Henry VIII to the death of George III.

A letter from Rev. Bull, the Vicar of 1870 states that the new school was built for 125 children but had an average attendance of 85. He also reveals that the old workhouse had been used as the parish school for several years past, when it was 'under government inspection'. In his letter he is proposing that the old workhouse dining room should become an extra classroom for 57 children, partitioned off to allow access to an upstairs room that 'used to be a girls school but is now a cottage'. He says that he, as Vicar, is the 'occupier' of the property given by the Patron of the Living and Lay Impropriator Sir Charles Goring, Bart. of Highden, Steyning, as long as Sir CG lives for the benefit of the schools. The income from cottage and garden rent are presently commuted to pay the school expenses. He seems reluctant to miss the opportunity of the extra school places, while recognising no immediate need, but fearful that if asked to build, presumably on the new school, he could not find the necessary £100, as indeed it was, in 1912.

The modern Junior and Infant schools, which for many years had separate buildings, staff and Governors in Station Road, were finally amalgamated in 2010.

1866

The Chancel at St. Mary's was rebuilt and a new font installed.   The restoration work was paid for by Henry Carnsew of Summers together with two new stained glass windows. Luke Wadey and Owen Voice, local craftsmen, did the work.

The Victorian regeneration

1867

Two pieces of land were assigned involving Sarah Durham, widow, Peter Evershed, surgeon, and Henry Wells, Horsham, builder. In this year mantraps formerly used at Rowfold Orchard were abandoned.

United Reformed Church

1868

In 1868 Philip Puttock in his will bequeathed £343.16, invested in Consuls, the dividend to be paid to the Vicar and Churchwardens to distribute in bread to the poor of the parish. John Ireland left £91.14s, also in Consuls to relieve the Church Rate.

The Congregational Church was erected on the corner of West Street. A school was added in 1885. The site was formerly part of a four and a half acre market garden. In 1972 it became the United Reformed Church. Non-conformists had met under licence at Peter Draper's private house in Billingshurst after the Indulgence

Act of 1672 but it was not until 1815 that a church with premises was founded by John Croucher of Hayes. He bought up the redundant octagonal officers' mess at Horsham used by the military gathered to resist a possible invasion by Napoleon. He had it rebuilt in Jengers Meadow, on a site now to the rear of the Jengers Mead shopping precinct as a meeting place for Presbyterians in Billingshurst. The Old Chapel and the cottage next door at Jengers were sold in 1889 and the adjoining Manse was then built on the new site. There is a memorial to the Rev. William Wilson M.A. who was ejected from the Parish Church at the Restoration under the 'oppressive Act of Uniformity'.

A 1680 sq yd plot in the south west corner of the Bowling Alley, then a five acre pasture field, was noted as ' in the possession of Henry Carnsew of Summers Farm and on it are erected a schoolroom, playground and master's garden'. On its south boundary is the Workhouse, owned by Sir Charles Goring and a piece owned by a Mr. Sadler of Chiddingfold and occupied by Sprinks, the miller. Sadler also has the land to the West of the plot. The remainder of the Bowling Alley is part of Duckmore farm, owned by Mr. Carnsew. The request was for a conveyance to the Vicar and Churchwardens for use as a Sunday School'

1871

The 1871 census reveals that William Sprinks was now aged 62 and married to Ruth, 52. He was now farming 140 acres and employing 5 labourers and a boy. He had three live-in servants, all about 18 years of age- John? Ervine, Henry Lellicot and Elizabeth Barnett.

Three families then lived at the Workhouse, four Lelliots and a lodger, two Reeds and a lodger, the Burchells with eight children and the Wilsons with two children and two lodgers. All were manual workers, woodcutters, farm labourers, gardeners, washerwomen, bricklayers' labourers.

At an auction at the Kings Arms James Wilson 'of Gratwick House', a civil engineer, bought Lockyers for £1090 from Trustees Farhall and Clear. A mortgage document (for £3500) suggests that 'a capital messuage' called Gratwick House with outbuildings a garden and orchard had formerly been occupied by Henry Carnsew, owner of Summers Place. It had been built on the site of a place named 'Hill House'. There was an adjoining messuage and stable.

In 1882 James Wilson bought Robin and Chime cottages.

Robin and Chine cottages

Hard times and good times

1874 +

This year marks the onset of the late Victorian agricultural depression. Cheap bread occasioned by imported wheat from Canada and America, and meat from the colonies and new world combined to undermine farming profits. Only dairy products, hay and horticultural fruit and vegetables could compete successfully with the overseas products of more favourable climates and soils. But in other respects the national economy was booming, with great fortunes falling to the well-to-do in banking, industry and trade with the Empire, while the yeoman farmers often faced bankruptcy. There were three such misfortunes in East Street alone. The numerous children of the poor often enough took off for the towns, the lads to find industrial and mechanical work and the girls a place in domestic service. Yet more bade farewell to their Billingshurst relatives and went off to Canada, Australia, Africa and New Zealand to seek a better fortune.

However rich town-dwellers, then as now, relished a 'place in the country' where they could relax or retire and enjoy the romance of the country-side and indulgence in rural sports, angling, hunting, the dog and the gun. Town money came to the rescue of the countryside. For example four substantial country mansions were established in Billingshurst bringing with them the wealth of their incoming owners and the opportunities for employment that their coming occasioned. There were hunting facilities for those with a taste for it and enough money and leisure to indulge it. There were Lord Leconfield's and Crawley and Horsham packs. The Warnham Staghounds worked Billingshurst and had point-to-points at Lordings Farm. Mr. Goff at Wooddales Farm had beagles. One of his followers was Dr. W.G.Grace, the famous cricketer.

Not the least of these benefits was the restoration work on St. Mary's Church and the building of the School in East Street. It is noticeable that though there is much sounder older building in the village and also much good Victorian property, nevertheless little remains to us from the Georgian period.

The coming of the railway had brought benefits for traders. Wooden hoops for barrels were exported by Henry Puttock from the Hoop Sheds by the station. Coppicing of hazel chestnut, ash and beech every seven years was a regular source of employment. The hoops were used for binding barrels, mainly for fishermen, but also for sugar, crockery barrels and tea chests. Carter Bros of Newpound built and sold their famous Unique straw elevator and industries such as the Gas

Works, Keating's Flea Powder manufactory and The Whirlwind Vacuum Cleaner factory, which made 400 machines a week, were able to flourish. The latter was built on the site of a malting in Station Road. It became Barralets Water Heaters in 1947 and is now Weald Court housing development. The American factory-owner, Mr. N.Ray Stiles, occupied Broomfield Lodge where Mr James King, the maltster once lived. He had the wall built that defines the former village cricket field in Station Road

These are emblematic changes. What had once been a farming village with a few shops for meat and groceries, bakers, shoes, clothes and basic everyday goods, with coaching inns and maltings, began to take on its present identity as a small marketing place and a dormitory, social and religious centre with light industry and service providers such as estate agencies, restaurants and secondary schooling for an extensive rural catchment. Mrs. Lines, local historian, has established that four shops paid rent to the church in the 15th century. The middle years of the 19th brought an explosion of shop-keeping enterprise and an expansion of retailing by independent traders once they had ready access to wholesale suppliers. This entrepreneurial spirit has continued. One chain store, International Stores, appeared between the wars, but it has been only recently that national supermarket chains such as Budgens, Tesco and Scats have offered a challenge to independent businesses offering groceries, clothing, confectionary, ironmongery, computer services, and the like.

The Station Road Malting before conversion to a factory

1874

The Sussex Directory listed Wm. Sprinks as a farmer at Hoile Farm. He appears to no longer be the miller probably having retired. One H. Isted takes over, followed quite soon by W.F.Weller -1878.

1876

In this year the first great Ordnance Survey map was issued showing all the fields and woods. The accompanying book gave acreages and use as arable or pasture.

The signal box at Billingshurst Station was re-erected since it was built much earlier. It is now a listed building as it is the only remaining example of the first standard box designs.

1881

The census of 1881 shows that William Sprinks then farmed only 26 acres. He had two 17 year old servants, Mary Lindfield and Thomas Redman.

1884

The clock at St.Mary's, a half size replica of the clock at Westminster, was installed. A year before an organ had replaced a harmonium. Earlier there had been a musician's gallery prior to the 1866 renovations.

1885

The Manor of Pinkhurst reported in 1881 that Thomas Trower had died, who 'held freely the messuage and land upon which the Mill is erected'. 'He had no animal'. Edward Underwood of Billingshurst, miller, now held the premises. 'Fealty respited'.

William Sprinks, the old miller, of East Street died. He was buried at the Baptist Chapel

1890

Pinkhurst Manor reported: Edward Underwood, freehold, Hammonds or Cocks Brook.

1891

The following year Ruth Sprinks, nee Older died aged 73.

The next census in 1891 listed Edward 48 and wife Mary Underwood 42, farmer with servant Annie Blate 19 as in occupation of Hammonds. Edward died in 1923 aged 80.

Four Wilsons were still at the Workhouse cottages, but William and Ellen Lintott, (pale cleaver) with 3 sons and a stepson, Hale and Lucy Goodyer (carpenter) with 5 children and John Ewins (scripture reader) and Emma his seamstress daughter had replaced the previous tenants.

James Wilson, his wife Cecelia, Margery his stepdaughter and three servants were at Gratwick House but not for much longer.

In 1895 the sweeps of the mill were badly damaged when in charge of an apprentice.

1901

By the time of the 1901 census Emma Ewins, spinster, was in three rooms at the Old Workhouse as caretaker of the Working Men's Club. The club was founded about 1880. It had 150 members with Honary Secretaries, named Wright, Headmaster at the School, and Peacock in 1885, succeeded by Joseph Luxford, shopkeeper, until 1915. It was housed for two years at the old Village Hall in 1911. The members of the club no doubt had a hand in the 'firing of the anvil' ceremonial explosion in 1900 to celebrate the relief of Ladysmith during the Boer War. A long fuse of gunpowder led to a heavy charge packed under the smith's anvil where it was fixed to the block. When ignited it produced a satisfactory roar! It was traditional to celebrate 'Old Clem Night' in this way on 23rd November. St. Clement was the patron saint of blacksmiths.

Working Men's club building, Library Car Park, now a greengrocer's

A purpose-built Working Men's Club was later erected in 1913 behind the Post Office off the High Street, the land being the gift to the village of Major General Renton J.P, DSO, OBE, DL, fruit farmer and horticulturist, of Rowfold Grange. In 1949 it had 200 members and plans for expansion. It later became a Social Club but afterwards declined and finally petered out at the Millennium. It is now a Farm Shop and Restaurant.

1901

Death of Queen Victoria – the 20th Century

Edward T Norris, 45, a rich brewer from Hertfordshire, bought Gratwick House in 1898. His wife was Jessie. They kept a butler and four servants in house with a stableman and gardener living in the stables. Sir Edward Lutyens designed a billiard room added on to the ostentatious building.

The body of Queen Victoria passed through Billingshurst Station on its way from the Isle of Wight to London in 1901

The village population was 1591 only 50 more than in 1840. Farming had been in depression since 1874 and few new employment opportunities were yet available.

Post Office

1902

The village Post Office was built with a plaque with an E for Edward VII. Now it is just a delivery office.

Looking East, with Hammonds Mill and St. Mary's on the skyline

Mr Malcolm Laker recorded notes of a conversation with Herbert Laker about the picture of Billingshurst taken from what is now Mill Lane. This abridged version adds colour to the Billingshurst scene in Edwardian days.

"Uncle Tom Laker bought the orchard from Mr. Ireland and this became the car park and library after it was sold to the Council. There was a barn at the corner of the lane now beside the Post Office. Uncle Tom bought the barn and first built his house on the site and then he built the shops and the bank, now a solicitor's office. The horse in the picture would have belonged to Willy Puttock who moved to Stonepits in Marringdean Road.

The barn in the picture is probably behind the Puttock's house in the High Street [Carlton House soon to become three shops]. The house on the left of the Church belonged first to Arnolds – the grocer, then to Billy Shepherd who took one of the shops that Uncle Tom built and then Billy sold to Walker's Stores. [Now an estate agents].

The Six Bells is on the right and the white house on the extreme right was at the top of the ten steps, a coal merchant lived there. Just left of the white chimneys is the dark side of the old barn which Tom bought. Where Rice Bros garage was (Budgens now) there was a red building which had been a grain store. Sid Streeter bought it and started a garage which Rice Bros took over. Sid did 18 months for fraud (some of this is libellous!). His mother lived in Bowling Alley Lane [Little East Street]. The poplar trees on the right are where the toilets are now.

The grocer's shop [on the corner of East Street, now a Chinese restaurant] was a blacksmith's shoeing shop belonging to Mr. Cook who emigrated to Australia. There was another baker's at the corner of Bowling Alley Lane, next door was a chemist's, then George Ware the draper, next 'Twinkle' Quick's the bicycle shop and then Henry Foice the butcher.

Other places in the village were Nellie Puttock's house who lived at Clevelands with her sister and Wildens bought by Teddy Norris, the brewer. Willy Puttock sold the big house that is Knights to an American [Ray Stiles] who bought the old malt house and built the factory for vacuum cleaners on the site.

There was a footpath from half way along the church walk [now under Carpenters] that came out on the main road by a saw pit used by Mr. Wadey who was the wheelwright on the corner of Newbridge Road [West Street] Opposite the Croft, another Laker's house, there was a private school where 'Grampy Laker' went to school, now a restaurant.

Rev. Stanley built a hut for the boy scouts in the grounds of the Vicarage before the First World War. Billy Renton of Rowfold made a donation for the Working Men's Club and Joe Luxford who had the sweet shop [on the East Street corner] went round collecting for the rest of the money. Joe had tennis courts in the allotments."

The village allotments, nearly five acres, began after the Great War. Another interesting business was basket-making from osiers grown at what is now Dell Lane. There stood three ponds and a dammed stream to nourish the willows.

Younger readers will not remember the retailing culture that still prevailed in Billingshurst up to the 1960s. Shopkeepers, often eminently recognisable personalities, displayed their goods safely on shelves behind stout counters where the scales and cutting and wrapping equipment stood. The shop assistants proffered sample goods on request, the customer made a decision, cash or a cheque changed hands, the deal was registered in a mechanical till and the goods were handed over, having been packaged from bulk on the spot by the seller. The system was economical of packaging and risk. It demanded a respectful personal relationship between vendor and customer, but was labour intensive and time consuming for both the management and customer. Goods had to be measured or weighed and priced, then wrapped. Customers had to wait patiently while others were served. The absence of refrigeration too made frequent shopping obligatory, since even outdoor meat safes and cool larders were unreliable safeguards against decay. Limited independent car ownership also favoured local village shopping. Groceries were often ordered in advance and delivered by rounds men on trade bikes or in a, horse-drawn or motorised van. Bread vans, milk floats and door-to-door salesmen visited local streets and remote farms alike. The old system still continues in independent butchers, greengrocers, shoe shops, jewellers and other specialised outlets, but elsewhere, even for bulky and expensive items like boxed TV sets or containerised Christmas trees the 'supermarket principle' prevails.

Profits soared and the traditional shopkeepers could not match the supermarket prices. The system is fast, efficient, gives generous choice and must make economic sense, but it lacks the warmth and human interaction of the old way which afforded employment for many more people than today's less personal experience, where a trolley load of goods may be purchased without the exchange of a single word.

The first English supermarket was in 1948, but the new retail culture in Billingshurst came in the 1970s.

1906

Rev Stanley gave the Old Village Hall to the parish. The derelict East Windmill was badly damaged beyond repair by a gale. The hand-winded wooded cap was blown off. The following year the Gas Works was built.

Billingshurst's Heritage

1. Frank Patterson

2. Drawing by Frank

1909

Kelly's Directory of 1909 gives more interesting details of the village shortly before the Great War. The chief landowners were said to be the trustees of the late Henry Puttock of Carlton House, Mr. Goff of Wooddale who had Summers Place built, Mr. Shepley-Shepley, Mr. Schroeter and two Irelands of Manor House and Broomfield. Edward Ireland was Lord of the Manor of Bassetts Fee. The Duke of Norfolk held the Manors of Pinkhurst and Storrington. The Misses Beck are at Duncan's Farm, Norris at Gratwick, Maj. General Renton, subsequently Chairman of Governors at the Weald School, at Rowfold Grange, Ephraim Wadey, undertaker and brickmaker at Parbrook, James Wadey, builder was at Five Oaks, Frank Arnold the Grocer at Churchgate, Ellen Chart ran a girls' day school, George Coombes farmed at Frenches, Mr. Crisp was the hairdresser, Mr. Foice was the butcher, the Huberts were at Rose Hill, one a physician and surgeon, the other the public vaccinator, and Frank Patterson (b 1871), the celebrated 'cycling artist', lived at Pear Tree Farmhouse, a 16th century building, on the road to Barns Green. William Carter was collector of rates and Alfred Head collector of the King's taxes.

1911 To 1960s

Rev Stanley started the local Boys Scouts in a room over Rice's Garage then at the Vicarage. After the Great War the troop ceased for a decade but was revived in 1928. It prospered at Clevelands stables and flourished thereafter. 'Salvage' – mainly waste paper- was collected during WWII and messages run for the Home Guard and Civil Defence. Scouts and Guides still prosper at the Scout Hut on the Recreation Ground.

The Billingshurst Band began in 1919, promoted by Mr. Luxford. The Miss Becks paid for the instruments and the uniforms. Sadly the band went into decline in the 1950s and the instruments were generously gifted to the Weald School, which had its own Wind Band.

Village events, such as the 1911 coronation party for George V following a floral parade, were held at Gratwick, the year Norris died. The family sold the estate in 1923. It was requisitioned during WW II. It then became a guest house. It fell into disrepair and was demolished in the early 60s to make way for Gratwicke Close, a row of well-designed terrace houses with garages, characteristic of the period. Specimen trees were planted on the green fronting East St.

Also in 1911 Dr. Hubert gave up his practice of over forty years at Brick House which stood on the corner of East Street. Dr. Hubert's son took over at Rosehill. The Vet, Mr. J Craft moved into Brick House.

Brick House on the left of East Street

In the 15th century the Brick House site had been part of the Vicar's glebe. That oak framed house was built some time before 1635 when Henry Cooper, a maltster and inn owner used it and the adjacent croft as a maltings and brewery.

One of his inns was The King's Arms on the site of Lloyds Bank and he had mortgages on The Star and The White Horse Inn all three now long lost. His son Walter died about 1696 and was succeeded as maltster by Edward Laker who had married the Vicar Oram's daughter Ann. Edward and his widow were dead by 1719. The next maltster was Walter Longhurst, a Churchwarden. He was buried in 1768 by which time Richard Browne had taken over. He paid Land Tax for the Adversane malthouse too where first William Elmes then Charles Duke was in occupation. Maurice Ireland lived at Brick House from 1783. When Richard Browne died in 1787 his nephew, John Jefferies, had ownership.

By 1820 a relative, Jacob Caffin was paying the Land Tax and Peter Evershed, surgeon, apothecary and General Practitioner, was the occupant of the house and Henry Mitchell had the malthouse. Peter was a healthy doctor, dying in 1884 aged 91. Jacob Caffyn, a very wealthy gentleman of Cuckfield, died in 1850. He had extensive property in Cuckfield, Charlwood and Ditchling. His buildings and nursery in Billingshurst which was occupied by John Allman went to his son Thomas. The 'field and close of meadow' and the houses and malthouse occupied by Peter Evershed, Henry Mitchell, Matthew Caffin, Joseph Kensett, Powell, Chantler, Coleman and Lander he willed to his son James Caffin. However by 1859 Henry Mitchell had written in his diary 'I had to give up three public houses...Kings Head at Billingshurst...gave up the old wretched Malthouse I had used for many years in the High Street'.

Peter Evershed had retired by 1870 when William H Hubert took over the practice in partnership with George Laurance, an Irishman. Ann Gravatt was his servant and William Vinall, his groom. Later servants were called Gosden, Taylor, Balchin and Ayling, names still current in the village. By 1907 his son, William A. Hubert, was also practising from Rosehill which became the surgery. In 1929 Brick House was demolished and the Westminster Bank moved in 'although not quite out of the builder's hands' just in time for the Wall Street Crash!

In 1920 the Parish Council applied, unsuccessfully, for a speed limit of 10 m.p.h. for the High Street and 100 yards up East and West Streets.

By this time the derelict East Mill had lost the remains of the smock tower, burnt as it was unsafe, and the stone base was in use as a store.

The Hubert family

1933

In 1933 significant boundary changes added a large area north of Brinsbury College and west to the Arun to the parish of Billingshurst. Previously this land had been part of Pulborough.

1934

Electric street lighting, the first in England, came to Godalming in 1881, but it was not until the National Grid was in place that a new light dawned. From 1934 mains electricity had arrived in Billingshurst and people could light their homes with the turn of a switch rather than a paraffin or gas lamp and, in due course, power their new radios from the mains, rather than with 'accumulators' and dry batteries. In 1895 the Parish Council bought fourteen 50 candle powered paraffin lamps and paid Mr. Bristow, the lamplighter, 10 shillings a week 'moonlight nights excepted'. Gas was substituted in 1911. It has been argued that electricity was more significant for the villagers than the coming of the railway. Steam engines pulled the trains until 1938 when electrification was completed along the line. Early telephones also improved the lives of traders and better-off people. The telephone poles and multiple wires that lined almost all the roads are now scarcely remembered.

The advent of the automobile in growing numbers from the 1920s gave welcome scope for enterprising businesses in the trade, and a steady decline in the use of broughams, landaus, Victorias and horse-drawn hearses. When Mr. W.T.Voice, grocer and proprietor of a cab and horse service since 1822, died after WWII all his expensive old carriages were sold to dealers from Edenbridge for £21 the lot, loaded onto a train and hauled away. Some are said to have ended up as props at Elstree film studios.

The coming of public utilities is often overlooked though they transformed the working and social lives of the people and are today taken for granted until things go wrong. Piped water had arrived by 1911. The North Sussex Gas and Water Company set up a reservoir at what is now Old Reservoir Farm, and a waterworks between Groomsland and Gilmans Industrial Estate. Also, by 1911, a sewage works serving much of the village had been established at Parbrook by Horsham Rural District Council. People no longer had to dig a deep cess pit in the back garden to empty the bucket in their outdoor privy. The original sewage tank was de-commissioned when the new works, created in the late 60s, was given a major re-development in the 1980s.

1914-18 and '39-45

During 1918-19 The Old Workhouse was used to house German prisoners of war. In June 1918 a single church bell was tolled 50 times to commemorate the 50th Billingshurst man to be killed in the Great War.

Italian and German prisoners were encamped in Marringdean Road during WWII, now the site of a small housing estate called Kingsfold Close. An air-raid shelter for the schoolchildren was built in the corner of the field behind the Mill bordering the Bowling Alley. Three bombs fell, one off the High Street and two in fields east of the Mill. Evacuees came to the village from London and were lodged in family homes. Forty men volunteered for the Local Defence Volunteers in 1940. The Battalion of the Home Guard, as it became, numbered 500 by 1944. They paraded at the old Village Hall with Battalion Headquarters at Gratwicke. The Royal Observer Corps kept watch for hostile aircraft at a post just beyond East Street. A painted board is still in place there, said to have been a device which would change colour if there were a gas attack. Boys learned aircraft recognition and made model aeroplanes and older ones joined the village Air Cadets, many of

The Home Guard March Past in the High Street

whom later became RAF aircrew. They collected acorns for pig food and conkers used for making acetone for which they were paid 7s-6d a cwt. Admiral Holmes and Mr. Maille led a team of Air Raid Wardens. They distributed and fitted 3000 gas masks, billeted the evacuees, organised emergency feeding arrangements, and trained 500 people in fire guard duty. Land girls worked on the farms and were trained at Brinsbury. The Whirlwind Factory in Station Road was given over to making ammunition boxes.

At Coolham an airstrip opened up to support the D-day landings of 1944. Large numbers of troops were assembled in Sussex ready for the assault on Normandy. In Billingshurst, Ingfield Manor was the Headquarters of the 1st Corps with a Royal Artillery Regiment, Infantry Workshops, a RAMC Casualty Clearing Station and two RASC Ordnance Ammunition Companies. At Wooddale was gathered another RA Regiment and a Royal Engineers Port Operating Company. Similar RE Companies were at Tedfold and Rosier Farm in a tented camp.

The Billingshurst Fire Brigade dates from 1938 and an Auxiliary Fire Service was formed. During WWII twelve firewomen were recruited and 50 fires due to enemy action were attended. In 1948 the Brigade was taken over from the Rural District Council by The County Council and re-equipped. In 1953 the present Fire Station, unlucky number 13, was built with Cecil Rhodes as the Station Commander and a total staff of 23.

Raymond Cecil Rhodes, centre, with the Fire Brigade staff

Evacuees arriving at the Station from Oliver Goldsmith School, Camberwell

Post-war Billingshurst

The most striking changes to the village since 1945 have been the growth of housing and population. Decade by decade there have been fresh estates established. In the 1960s Jengers Mead was transformed into a shopping precinct, parking space and flats. Subsequently estates were developed east of Silver Lane and on the sites of former Glebe Land, Gratwick and Clevelands. The factory in Station Road was developed into Weald Court and Saville Gardens and another cluster of houses built off Forge Way in the west.

A remarkable, though strangely unremarked, contrast between village life in 1912 and in 2012 is the divergence of the people who conduct the trading business of the village and the people who make their homes there. A hundred years ago the pillars of the community were the shopkeepers and traders, often members of long-standing local families, such as those elected to the first Parish Council. Today only a single member runs a business in the village. Then most proprietors lived 'over the shop' or within walking distance of it.

Today a good many of them live elsewhere and several big shops are branches of chain stores run by managers. If they do not live in the village they naturally have a loyalty to their home place, its school, church and other social circles. Their 'roots' are therefore not in Billingshurst. In 1912 not only the shopkeepers but also the schoolteachers, the doctors and nurses who made home visits, the factory owners, the policemen, the station staff, the roadmen, the builder, the butcher and the baker, and most people offering services lived in the village and were likely to add 'and Sons' to their title, as a emblem of continuity. Such a quintessential civic figure as Joe Luxford epitomised an undivided spirit of committed citizenship typical of the old order. Today only Rhodes, the cobblers, have maintained the independent shop tradition. There are modern exceptions of course. The Vicar, the publicans, the ethnic restaurateurs and farmers still have a rational interest in dwelling in the place where they earn their living.

The obverse of the rule also applies. Many of the families now domiciled in the village earn their living elsewhere, Gatwick, Crawley, the coastal towns or London, and may well do their shopping and seek their entertainment somewhere other than Billingshurst. Fortunately many employees of local enterprises are still recruited locally to the benefit of the community spirit of the village. Nevertheless we must conclude, for better or worse, the railway, the bus service and most tellingly the motor car have created a 'commuting society' in Billingshurst just as significant as anywhere else in Britain. It is an inescapable fact that, in a mobile society, a great many people now living in Billingshurst were not born and brought up there. It is not surprising that the interests of the Chamber of Commerce sometimes conflict

Billingshurst's Heritage

with those of the domiciliary residents. The latter tend to prefer to safeguard their exclusiveness and restrict expansion, the former look for growth and more potential customers.

In the mid 1990s, after forty years of delay and prevarication, a Western by-pass was built, and 550 new residences constructed within its boundary. This major expansion brought with it assets to boost the infrastructure at the developer's expense. Billingshurst gained the £8M by-pass, an all-weather pitch at the Weald School, educational funding, a new village hall or Community Centre and enhancements to the High Street, extensive sports facilities at Jubilee Fields and the Swimming Pool and Leisure Centre. More recently blocks of flats have risen near the Station and infilling with small estates has occurred wherever the District Council could be persuaded to grant planning permission. Five instances of this are off East Street alone. Apart from the older Rosehill development houses have been built at Caffyns Rise, off School Lane, at Luggs Close, in the grounds of Trees and at Hammonds Garden Field. Similarly six small estates have been permitted branching from the High Street and another off Forge Way. More details of post-war developments are shown in Appendix 1.

The pavilion at Jubilee Fields

Three industrial zones offer some employment to an ever increasing population. However where there were once four garages, filling stations and car showrooms in the High Street and a coach depot, all of these have now succumbed to alternative development so that the traditional function of Billingshurst as a coaching inn centre and transport hub is no longer so since the building of the western by-pass which relieved the High Street of the former intolerable traffic congestion in the summer months.

1966

In 1966 Mary Constance Trower died aged 82 and two years later, in 1968 Gertrude Amy Trower died aged 77. Both sisters had lived at Hammonds.

At an auction at Horsham Town Hall, offered for sale by the executors of Gertrude Trower of Hammonds, was 'a house of character, part-built in the 17th century, 4 bedrooms, bathroom, 2 dressing rooms, attic bedroom, entrance hall, 2 reception rooms, scullery, kitchen, store rooms, etc. Garage and barn.' The remainder of the estate continued in the ownership of the Trower Trustees who act in the interest of the heirs who live abroad. The fields have been let to tenant farmers for many years, and at the time of this writing is the subject of an application for a major development scheme by a consortium of building companies.

1969

The house and garden was bought by Dr. Evelyn Kilsby whose surgery was beside St. Mary's church.

1983

It was subsequently bought by John Griffin.

A steam engine entering Luggs Yard off East Street

James Lugg, a previous apprentice at Carter Bros. of Newpound, agricultural engineers, founded a threshing tackle and traction engine business on the northern side of East St. opposite to what was once called Lockyers Farm, and just west of the old Workhouse. This is now a small housing estate called Luggs Close.

The Bowling Alley in winter

The Bowling Alley, north of Hammonds, now a wooded scrubland, was used for sledging and by the schoolchildren for ball games. Gratwicke House south of East St. was built about 1830 and substantially enlarged by Edward Norris. After WWII it was used for band practice and for a while provided premises for a fish and chip shop! It was demolished in the 1960s and an estate, Gratwicke Close, was built on the site. Gratwicke Lodge and the stable block still remain, as do Robin and Chime Cottages, built in the 18th century or earlier. Churchgate, a 17th century timber-framed house, had a shop wing added in Victorian times when Billy Shepherd was known, at 18 stone, as the fattest grocer in Sussex. It was later a guest house.

More recent developments

1977

After General Renton's death Rowfold Grange was sold and the mansion split into three apartments.

Aerial photograph to celebrate the Queen's Jubilee in 1977.

1. The Weald School from the air showing buildings and a tribute to the Queen at her Silver Jubilee

Rowfold Grange today

1978

Cleveland House, formerly the Puttock family home, was demolished to make way for affordable housing.

Shortly after this the Billingshurst Bonfire Society ceased, though the celebration of Guy Fawkes has recently been revived at Jubilee Fields. 'The Bonfire Boys' used to meet at the Six Bells. They staged the main event at Ireland Hill, the SCATS or Junior School sites, or a field at the end of Daux Avenue. The preliminary procession, headed by the Village Silver Band would start at the Old Village Hall where the Fancy Dress Competition was judged, circumnavigate the village via the High Street, Natt's Lane and the Station, finishing at the chosen venue, but stopping at every pub en route. Other Societies, The Haven, Adversane, New Pound, Loxwood, Shamley Green etc. would pay reciprocal visits so that participants were drunk for a week! The Bonfire Prayer would be said and the fire lit. Rabbits would emerge as they did when a field of corn was cut, as the pyre was prepared months in advance.

Bonfire Boy William Phillips as 'Old Bill', WW I cartoon character, by Bruce Bairnsfather

1987

In the early hours of Friday, October 16th 1987 a 120 m.p.h. gale swept through southern England. Access roads to Billingshurst were blocked, all trains cancelled and power supplies cut off for ten days or more. Food stored in freezers thawed out and shopkeepers sold off their deteriorating goods, candles lit the homes and chain saws chattered on all sides. Roofs were smashed in, cars crushed and the face of the church clock, which dates from 1884, was blown out. East Street and Station Road were impassable. Great areas of woodland and scores of magnificent old trees were uprooted. 40,000 trees were said to have fallen across traffic routes in West Sussex alone. Chanctonbury Ring was devastated and half the specimen trees at Wakehurst Place and Nymans Gardens were ruined. National insurers paid out £2 billion.

1. Fallen tree by Silver Lane blocking Station Road

2. Tower minus clock

3. fallen clock face at St. Mary's church

2011

Summers Place was restructured as apartments with a housing estate in the grounds.

1. Unrestored Mill barn

2. Today

Studies have proved that there are still twenty or more 16th and 17th century timber-framed houses and inns in good order in the village and eighty in the neighbourhood, whereas the more pretentious grand houses erected in Victorian times like Gratwick and Clevelands have succumbed to modern housing and Summers Place has been massively reordered. These premises were too expensive to maintain and stood in valuable grounds, ripe for development. Of recent years a number of studies have been conducted to assist housing estate designers in the future and to describe the vernacular architecture characteristic of the village. The Village Design Statement of 2009 is extant. It tells of the familiar tile-hung elevations, using hand-made and decorative tiles, occasional use of horizontal timber cladding and the red brick walls with interspersed bricks in other colours. Causeway and Tithe cottage beside the Village Green were together an example of a classic Wealden house of the late 14th century. Much new development has echoed these traditional styles in appropriate modern machine-made materials.

St. Gabriel's Catholic Church, also in East St. was built in 1962 on a site gifted by Mr. and Mrs. Maille of Marringdean Rd. some twenty years earlier. It was designed by Henry Bingham Turner of Uckfield and is described by local historian, Paul Smith, as 'in a watery Perpendicular style'. Pevsner judges it 'deplorable'. Tastes differ! The Mass had returned to Billingshurst, for the first time since the Reformation, in 1908 in a room over the late Cripps, the butcher's, in the High Street. The few catholic families who attended dwindled or moved away. Thirteen years later from 1925 about 40 Billingshurst and district Catholics worshipped in a building in Lower Station Road, originally The Gospel Hall, built in 1888 and used first by the Salvation Army and then the Plymouth Brethren. The

St. Gabriels Catholic Church

Hughes, Jukes and O'Reilly families gave generous help. Miss Shannon donated £100. From 1933 Fr. Walter Stone who became the resident priest boosted the growing congregation. He was followed by Father Candy. By 1949 Sunday Mass was attended by 150 people in Pulborough and Billingshurst combined. A single brick wall with shallow arches is all that now remains of the Lower Station Road building.

When Hammonds Garden Field was excavated, prior to the granting of planning permission for housing in 2011, a great deal of late Victorian and early 20th century detritus was revealed – jugs, marmalade jars, bottles etc. It had obviously been used as an 'amenity tip' probably by East St. residents and other village people. Excellent dumping facilities are now sited at the entrance to Jubilee Fields sports grounds.

Opposite Mill Barn is 'Trees', a house of ancient appearance, but of recent construction made up from materials salvaged from demolitions of other properties by the late Harold Wadey, a notable member of a local building family founded by Ephraim Wadey in 1884.

Hammonds House and Hammonds and Little Daux dairy farm.

Hammonds is one of the old timber framed-houses in Billingshurst. The frontage to the A272 has a classic Horsham stone roof and a brick facade painted to keep the interior warm and dry. At the rear is an outdoor privy, still working, and a landscaped lawn and garden with a pond and two wells. The adjacent barn was partly demolished in the late 20th century but has been handsomely restored for ancillary use for the house. To the East are the restored remains of the old dairy farm buildings, converted in 1997 into a private house and renamed Mill Barn. The former milking parlour has been extended as a double garage and the calf sheds have become a secluded patio. The thick Horsham stone flooring of the derelict calf shed has been recycled as coping stones for a fish pond. The stackyard and farmyard is now an orchard and garden. In the years when it was a dairy farm a shed, still standing, fronted the road and was used to dispense milk to villagers either in cans or bottles printed with the Barnes Brothers trade mark. The dairy had its own well which still siphons water into a capacious Victorian brick-built L-shaped underground tank.

In 1931 Walter J Barnes and Sophie, his wife rented Hammonds Farm from the Trowers and Little Daux, from the Norris family of Gratwicke. The Barnes' had three sons, Jack, Leslie and Bob. Walter had kept a grocery shop at what is now the China Brasserie at the corner of East Street. They lived there for five years before moving into Little Daux. Leslie worked for a time on the farm, then became landlord at the Limeburners' Inn and then worked for King & Barnes, the Horsham brewers. Jack and Bob had a milk round, and their own eggs. They kept rabbits, pigs and horses and 15 milking cows at Hammonds, cows and calves at Little Daux and bullocks on land at Duckmore. They worked hard for a modest living, making hay and struggling with the clay, typifying a small mixed farm in Billingshurst. Bob died in 1988 by which time they had retired. Mrs. Barnes, Bob's wife, wrote a memoire of her life at Little Daux which illustrates what life was like on a Billingshurst dairy farm in the mid-20th century. Here is an abridged version of her account;

"I was courted by Bob when I worked at the Toat cafe on the way to Pulborough in 1952. He took me to the pictures at Horsham the day George VI died to see 'Lady Godiva'. We married the next year, a simple wedding with a three-tier wedding cake that they photographed. We spent the evening watching 'Jane Eyre' at the Royal Court theatre in Horsham. At Little Daux there was a long kitchen with a stone floor and a big wire-meshed safe for perishable food – no refrigeration then and a cellar which often flooded. The kitchen had a 4-burner oil stove and a copper over a fireplace to boil the laundry. The family's favourite food was mince and dumplings. No one ever opened the big front door and the 'big room' was reserved for visitors. Granddad would watch the weather over the station. 'It looked bad over Will's mothers'; he would say when rain threatened. One end of our house went back to the 15th century. You could see the Downs from the attic on a clear day.

We kept three dogs and 15 cats. Henry, my favourite kitten got run over by the oil lorry. Water was pumped across the football field, really Jubilee Field. When it froze up it came by churn from Hammonds. We had to boil up water on the stove to have a bath. The toilet was an Elsan in the garden – often full when visitors were coming, so we had to dig a hole quickly. 'Burying the dead' I called it. I was content with the lack of amenities. I never knew anything else.

We had daisies, irises, honeysuckle, climbing roses and Virginia creeper, Victoria plums, two greengages and a good vegetable garden. We had a milking machine in the garden driven by an engine. Muddles of Ashington brought the animal feed. Butcher, baker and grocers all delivered to the door. Jack got his day-old chicks from the station and reared them in brooders warmed by oil heaters. About three fields of the 40 acres of Little Daux would be shut up for making hay, usually the old-fashioned way by cart to ricks. Later we had a baler. We did not grow wheat or barley.

When baby Nick came I had no washing machine – just the Raeburn and a black pot. Ironing was done with small flatirons heated up on the stove, or even on the fire with a poker. Then I had a paraffin iron with meths in the front and a pump to get it going. Then we got electricity! Just enough from our generator for lights at first. When it broke down we were back to Tilly Lamps outdoors and Aladdins inside. When we got 'mains' we could have a cooker, an iron and a fridge. All the hedging was done with a chopper and swap hooks with bonfires along the hedgerows. At first Nan did the milk bottling and when Bob went to school his Dad would pass him in the van with the parrot in a cage at the back. They retired to School Lane in 1963 and Jack and Bob took over, Bob replaced the copper with the Raeburn which proved hard to master – many burnt offerings!

Bob loved hunting and following the hounds. One day Nick was lucky to survive when Bob backed the tractor out of the shed at Hammonds, knocking him over, luckily into a pile of manure! It saved his life. Dr. Hope-Gill fixed his broken collar-bone. The cows were a mixed herd – Friesians, Red Polls, Guernsey, Shorthorns and Sooty, the Jersey. Heifers were reared on to join the milking herd. The bullocks were kept for 18 months then went to market. Roger Green took them in his lorry. They were hard to load up. The air was blue sometimes.

Frank Kitchener worked as cowman. The women, Nan, Joyce, (Leslie's wife) and I washed the eggs that Jack's hens laid ready for the packing station; Leslie made cream for the milk round".

At the time of this writing a small estate is now occupied on the former orchard at Trees, fourteen houses are being constructed on Hammonds Garden Field to the rear of Hammonds House and to the south of the Bowling Alley. This steep area of woods and scrub is proposed to be refurbished as a public amenity and wildlife sanctuary.

Possible future developments

In 2001 the population of the parish was 6531, in 2012 over 7000, more than three times its total in 1830. It is likely to continue to rise. Not least of recent expansions has been the building of care homes, sheltered accommodation and residential closes specifically for the senior citizenry. These late 20th and 21st century developments have dropped windfall financial fortunes into the laps of those lucky Billingshurst citizens who owned title to land, or development companies that were shrewd enough to buy it up, where the lottery of planning legislation allowed the right to build expensive houses, at times when such building land was in short supply. Although unwelcome to many, vigorous representations are currently under discussion to permit another major expansion of 550 houses and community facilities on Duckmore, Cocksbrook and Couchers, This is despite Pevsner's judgement that, 'The Weald landscape near here is splendidly unspoilt, a continuously changing pattern of copses and small fields'.

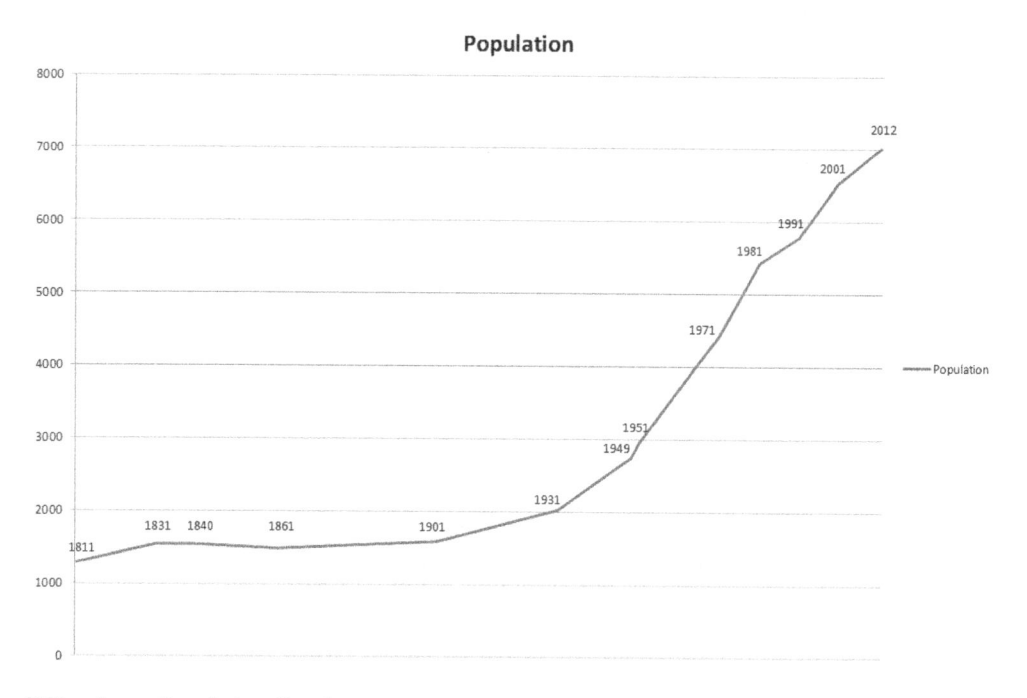

Billingshurst Population Graph

Billingshurst Characters and Celebrities

Most of the worthy public-spirited Billingshurst personages derived their deserved reputations in the annals of the village from their relative wealth, birth or office. Such leading citizens as the Greenfields, Puttocks, Sherlocks, Eversheds, Voices, Morris's, Lakers, Wadeys and Streeters leap to mind, not to mention the Gentry:- Goring, Ireland, Norris, Carnsew, Beck, Goff, and Renton; the entrepreneurs, Stiles, Wylde, Carter, Lugg and Merrikin; the shopkeepers, Crisp the hairdresser, Cripps the butcher, Lusted the grocer, Bernard Baker the outfitter, Gravett the confectioner, Jones the watchmaker, Rhodes the cobbler and Watts, the corn merchant at Hereford House by the Station. These are names that recur down the years, feature on the war memorial and are still to be found on the electoral roll. Many other well-remembered personalities are listed in the Appendices.

Numerous interesting characters have left their distinctive marks on the village history. One remarkable celebrity was Mr. Joseph Luxford, the Grand Panjandrum of the early 20th century. He was grocer and carrier, Secretary of the Working Men's Club, an original Parish Councillor, instigator of the building of the old Village Hall, sponsor of the Billingshurst Band, churchwarden, organiser of charabanc outings, actor in amateur dramatics, secretary of the Flower Show Committee, allotment owner and keen tennis player. He was surely the epitome of citizenship. Other remarkable figures included Henry and son, Buzzy Wright the schoolmasters, Dr. Moreton, master and actor, George Coombs, the oldest inhabitant, Frank Patterson the cycling artist and farmer, Billy Shepherd the fat grocer, Freddie Wells, angler, cricketer, gardener and Bonfire Society supporter, Dr. Hubert, G.P. and cricketer, Wally Wicks, champion gardener of Myrtle Cottages, Jack Leaman, Spike Milligan's commanding Officer and doyen of the British Legion, Jack Easton, Bank Manager and Chairman of the Parish Council, John and Renee Humphreys of the Dramatic Society, Lola Baxter ballet teacher at the Mission Hall, restaurateur and antiques dealer of Adversane and Hugh Wadey who saw Hammonds Mill collapse in a storm and kept his own museum of antiquities. Still flourishing are Cliff Griffin, ex-parish and district councillor and feisty business-man formerly of Poplar Garage, Five Oaks and Councillor Ken Longhurst who piloted the Western by-pass Committee. Nationally and rightly celebrated is the former West Sussex educational administrator, cycling tourist, author, wit and TV personality, Edward Enfield of Rowner and his gifted family which includes his son Harry, the comedian. Fondly remembered by passers-by was old William Richard. He was Mr. Ireland's shepherd and would station himself on Billingshurst Hill at weekends in his working clothes and decorated hat and salute travellers with his walking stick. Many other notable personalities are listed in the Appendices.

1. George Coombs

2. William Richard

The spirit of Billingshurst

The people of Billingshurst have long enjoyed their country sports as well as the familiar national games. Cricket had a long tradition at the ground in Station Road for some 180 years. Dr. Hubert was reputed to have struck a six on to the railway line and over the houses in Station Road. The ground is now superseded by excellent pitches at Jubilee Fields, created as a civic improvement when the Western by-pass was built, together with 550 new homes in the 1990s. Association football enjoys similar facilities after the club relinquished its Station Road pitch, originally created by the Parish Council from an old orchard. Plans are now being realised to create public gardens on these old sites where the new Children's Centre, Swimming Pool and Leisure Centre have left ample space. The old wall between the old pitches has been preserved but the derelict pavilion beside Station Road which originally stood on the south end next the Weald School boundary, has been demolished. The Weald School also furnishes playing fields for rugby football, a sports hall for basketball and a wide variety of other sports and games. The village boasts a thriving bowls club, founded in 1932 on land granted by Mrs. Alice Puttock, and it has a keen fraternity of anglers. The traditional Sussex ladies game of stoolball is no longer practised but lawn tennis is well provided for.

The oldest village club, the Horticultural Society is thriving. It has organised an annual show since 1882. There is a prospering Choral Society. The Billingshurst Dramatic Society, founded in 1941, stages remarkably proficient plays, thrice yearly, in the Women's Hall. Public spirited service clubs, the Lions and Rotary, give generous support to local good causes. The Lions staff a comprehensive bookshop and the Rotary, with the Scouts and Guides, stage an annual Village Show and Carnival Parade. The Women's Institute offers good companionship and in the 1950s created an excellent historical scrapbook to which this book is greatly indebted. The British Legion stages an annual Remembrance Day Parade, recalled by the War Memorial beside the ten Church Steps to the High Street, erected in 1921 commemorating 55 men who died in WWI and 9 in WWII.

The Parish Council meets in a handsome Community Centre in Roman Way which superseded the Old Village Hall in the High Street in 1991 before the opening of the western by-pass. It was built on a site that once had a hovel for cattle, converted into a house. The Council is active in the interest of the parish, together with its group of volunteers, known as the Community Partnership, which has a fine record of initiatives for the young, the elderly and the ordinary parishioners alike. There is a Fire Station manned by retained firemen and a conveniently sited branch of the County Library. The Village sign was erected in 1985 and The Heritage Plaque installed at the Millennium, 2000AD. Recent

The Village Community Centre, Roman Way

decades have seen, in the judgment of many, the building of more than enough accommodation for the care of the elderly but insufficient affordable housing for working families. Critics have also claimed to have lost count of the proliferating outlets for take-away meals and regret the struggle of independent shops to make a decent living. Six old inns continue to trade unlike the fate of many other public houses in the County and the Five Oaks Inn which has been demolished and replaced by automobile services. The pubs now depend on selling food as well as drink. However all the maltings which once nurtured the beer have long since disappeared. There are no longer any hotels since the Maltings Hotel and the last one at Adversane both closed but comfortable 'bed and breakfast' can be found and there is a motel at Five Oaks at what was once Jane's Tea Garden.

During the middle 20th century the character of Billingshurst High Street, as a coaching inn stopping place on an important road, persisted in that it hosted four automobile garages and a coach company selling cars, fuel and services. By the millennium the effect of the western by-pass, congestion and more remunerative uses for the sites of these premises has resulted in a migration of the businesses to the outskirts at North Heath and Five Oaks, or in the case of repair shops, to the Station area or one of the three industrial estates.

What then can be said of the broad characteristics of the people of Cocksbrook and of Billingshurst and district? Though it is dangerous, indeed ludicrous, to generalise too readily about a diverse and constantly fluctuating community of human spirits, nevertheless certain attitudes to life, politics and religion are sufficiently evident to invite a commentary if not an explanation. The Billingshurst spirit is best explained by what it is not. It has never been an especially wealthy community. It is not well endowed with rich soils and valuable minerals, nor affluent industries and accessible markets. Local yeoman farmers and traders have always struggled to make a decent living. They have, in consequence become

The Village War Memorial

independent, self-sufficient and enterprisingly self-reliant. Neither has it had the benefit of the benign influence of the affluent landed gentry. This contrasts sharply with vast swathes of rural West Sussex. There, time out of mind, the great, semi-feudal estates of Cowdray, Leconfield, Goodwood and the domain of the Dukes of Norfolk have determined much of the way of life of the people who tenanted their lands and serviced their communities.

But the people of Billingshurst, farmers, traders and cottagers alike, were obliged to be their own men, owning or renting their land, poor but free to differ, Sussex-wise, reluctant 'to be druv'. Although consistently loyal to the established Anglican Church, nevertheless important sectors of the people have long shown a dissenting spirit, displaying a rich tradition of chapel-going and 'do different'. The arrival of the Huguenots, Calvinist protestants seeking refuge from Catholic persecution in the 1560s and settling at Wisborough Green where they made glass, may well help explain this local divergence from the pro-catholic sympathies of Arundel to the south and the siting of a Quaker meeting house at the Blue Idol a mile up the road from East Street towards Coolham. Here William Penn, namesake of Pennsylvania, preached on his return from America in 1691. George Fox who founded the Meeting House was imprisoned in Horsham gaol for three months. A new Family Church, the fifth village congregation, has but recently been established.

The Blue Idol Quaker Meeting House off the road to Coolham

The Parish Council, since its statutory establishment in 1894, has earned itself a reputation for cantankerous debate, albeit with constructive initiatives for the well-being of the parishioners. In politics, similar to their stance in religion, the voters have consistently elected establishment-friendly Conservative Members of Parliament, yet unlike the rest of the wards of rural Sussex, they have shown a divergent spirit in their choice of County and District Councillors, even electing Liberal Democrats in the 1990s. The feminist movement too has enjoyed local support. In 1924 the Beck sisters of Duncans, Ellen and Edith, friends of Mrs Pankhurst and keen supporters of Women's Suffrage, bestowed The Women's Hall and the mothers' garden next door on the ladies of Billingshurst as a potent symbol of their independence of mind. The Women's Institute had first call on it. They undertook much charitable work for hospitals and other good causes and were particularly busy during WWII in support of the war effort and were still helping issuing ration books until they were discontinued in 1954.

Billingshurst's Heritage

The Firemen's Family Christmas Party at the Women's Hall, in the 1950s

Billingshurst is a village, trembling on the brink of becoming a town. Under an Act of 1974 the parish has the power to declare itself a Town Council, but the elected representatives continue to prefer a village status. Had it hosted a regular cattle market in times gone by, it might well have grown into a country town, a trading hub for its adjacent villages, a service it now provides in a modest fashion, in uncomfortable competition with Pulborough to the South and Horsham and Crawley to the North. Shopkeepers have struggled to profit from a relatively small 'footfall', though the population continues to expand, and shows every sign of continuing to do so. The conjunction of roads, the railway, the sporting and social clubs, swimming pool and fitness centre, the churches, banks, restaurants, supermarkets, workshops and light industries, a surgery, dentistry and vetinary surgeons, nursery and primary schools and the Weald Comprehensive Secondary School and Sixth Form College, all set in a rolling wooded countryside, combine to offer a rich environment to families who are fortunate enough to inherit the living space of their half-forgotten predecessors.

Acknowledgements

John Hurd, Wendy Lines and Paul Smith, three Billingshurst authoritative historians – invaluable advice and generous willingness to allow the use of their original research, maps and photographs.
Michael Jacob & Walter Parr – A Guide to Billingshurst Parish Church
Peter Brandon – The Sussex Landscape and The Kent & Sussex Weald
Wendy Lines -Billingshurst and Billingshurst and Wisborough Green
Malcolm Laker – Herbert Laker's memories
Geoff Rhodes – advice and photographs
Duncan Reynolds – photograph advice and research
John and Terry Griffin – meticulous proof-reading and the liberty of their 'Hammonds messuage'
Billingshurst, West Sussex – Parish Guide
Billingshurst Women's Institute – Scrap Book, prepared in the 1950s in collaboration with the Parish Council
W.E. Tate – The Parish Chest
E.V. Lucas Highways and Byways: in Sussex
Tony Wales – A Sussex Garland
The Blue Idol – www.blueidol.org.uk
Rev Arthur Young – A General View of the Agriculture of Sussex 1813
R. Thurston Hopkins – Old English Mills and Inns 1927
Debora Evershed –From Hadfoldshern.....to Adversane
Valerie Porter – The Village Parliaments
David Arscott -Philips County Guide to West Sussex
Martin Brunnarius – The Windmills of Sussex
G.M. Trevelyan – English Social History and other similar social and economic works by notable historians, Simon Schama, Asa Briggs, P. Sauvain, Richard Humble, Sean Lang, G.E. Mingay and Christopher Hibbert
West Sussex Records Office
Billingshurst, Storrington and Horsham Libraries
Roger Birch – Sussex Stones
Tim Churchill, Paul Smith and Julie Barnes for permission to use photographs and original research
Google Search and Wikipedia
The Billingshurst Community Partnership – Historical leaflet
Peter Ethrington – loan of Ross Booklet
Advice on many topics – Peter Lines, Kim Hope, Des Wakeling, Alastair Morris, Roger Patterson, Gillian Yarham, Eric Clark, Durwin Banks, Ann Brooks, My

daughters, Sarah Moloney, research and technical assistance, and Lucy Archer, cover design.

My wife Gilly for her patience and frequent technical first-aid.

Appendix 1 Housing development

Compiled by Mr. Paul Smith

Builders at work in 2012 on 'Windmill Close' – The Garden Field at Hammonds

BILLINGSHURST ROADS AND ESTATES				
Street Name/ Development	Date Built & Notes	Developer/ Builder	Comment	Named After
Amberley Court, Brooker's Road	2002-03	Bellway Homes		After Amberley village
Anvil Close	1976	Horsham DC		After Forge that stood on corner of W & High Streets
Arun Court, Rosehill	1988-89	Vinall		River Arun
Arun Crescent	2009	Saxon Weald	6 Eco Houses	River Arun
Arun Road & Flats	E 1960's	Horsham RDC	Flats rebuilt	River Arun
Arundel Court, Brooker's Road	2002-03	Bellway Homes		After Arundel town
Barrow Close	2000-01	Taywood Homes	Penfold Grange Dev Phase 3 & 4	Penfolds owned Gilmans in the early 17th Century
Belinus Drive	1974-76	Sunley Homes		After Roman surveyor of Stane Street
Berrall Way N	1999-2000	Taywood Homes	Penfold Grange Dev Phase 1 & 2	Local family, landowning gentry
Berrall Way S	2000-02	Taywood Homes	Penfold Grange Dev Phase 3 & 4	Local family, Stanmore Late 19th Century
Birch Drive - W end	E 1960's			Birch trees line much of the road
Birch Drive - E end	1970-71	Sunley Homes		name continued from W end, but few trees!

Bridgewater Close	1998-99	Shared Ownership		
Brookfield Way	c.1971			Plot adjoins Par Brook stream
Broomfield Drive	1970-71	Sunley Homes		After barn and cottage nearby (Pennybrooks)
Caffyns Rise	L 1990's			After a local landowner and Surveyor
Carpenters	1966-67	Croudace	62 properties	Field Name
Cedars Farm Close	1976	Horsham DC		From The Cedars (Farm)
Cherry Tree Close	M 1960's			Tree name
Chestnut Road - East End	1987-88			Tree name
Chestnut Road - West End	L C19 - E C20			Tree name
Cleve Way	E 1960's		Clevelands was demolished in 1978	
Clevelands	1978-79	Chichester Diocesan Housing Association		After C19 house on site
Coombe Close	L 1980's			
Coombe Hill	L 1940's - E 1950's	Horsham RDC		
Cranham Avenue	1998-99	Westbury		Upholstery shop-keeper 1880 ?
Daux Avenue	1900's Onwards	Various/Davis		After Farm and nearby wood
Dauxwood Close	1981	Charles Wadey & Sons		Daux Wood lies behind road
Dell Lane	1979-80	Fairclough Homes		In a dip!
Downsview Cottages, West Street	L 1930's	Horsham RDC		Did have a view of the South Downs!
Easton Crescent	L1990's - 2010	Gleeson Homes		After Cllr Jack Easton, long time chairman of Parish Council
Farriers Close	1982	Hilbery Chaplin		Relating to the Forge in the High Street
Forge Way - N end	L 1960's			After Forge that stood on corner of W & High Streets
Forge Way - Middle Section	1976	Horsham DC		After Forge that stood on corner of W & High Streets
Forge Way - E end	1974-76	Sunley Homes		After Forge that stood on corner of W & High Streets

Name	Date	Developer	Notes	Origin
Forge Way - SW spur	1983	Horsham DC		After Forge that stood on corner of W & High Streets
Forge House, West Street	E 1980's		Converted L 1990's from offices to flats	Site of forge and wheelwright's shop
Freemans Close	1974-76	Sunley Homes		Possible local name
Frenches Mead	L 1940's - E 1950's	Horsham RDC		After Farm that stood to the W
Freshlands	2002-03	Bryant Homes/ Taylor Woodrow	Penfold Grange Dev Phase 5	
Gorselands	1978-80	Gleeson Homes		
Gratwicke Close	L 1960's			After house the stood here called Gratwicke
Griffin Close	2012	Sunninghill Construction/ Saxon Weald	Architect - Kenn Scadden Associates	
Groomsland Drive	1939, E 1950's	Horsham RDC		After Groomsland Farm that stood to the NW
High Seat Gardens	E 2000's			After High Seat, house nearby
High Street (Behind 82a)	2011-12	Now called Lauras's Garden	4 Mews houses on site of Slaughterhouse	
Hillview Court	2010	Taylor Wimpey	14 Properties	After former Garage named Hillview that was on site
Holders Close	2005-06	Bryant Homes/ Taylor Woodrow	Newbridge Gardens Dev	Familiar local name
Hurstlands	1974			After house on site
Jengers Mead shops with flats above	L 1960's		Gingers house stood beside the Maltings	Jengers is a corruption of Gingers
Jengers Mead - NE Quadrant	1999-2000			
Jubilee Court, High Street	2002	McCarthy & Stone	Formerly Billingshurst Coaches yard	Developer's name
Kenilworth Place, Natts Lane	2004	David Wilson Homes	Brooklands Place Dev	After previous house on site built in 1930's
Kingsfold Close	1988-89		Prisoner of war camp, then a riding stables	After nearby house of Kingsfold
Kingsley Mews, Brooker's Road	M 1990's			
Lakers Meadow	1988-89			Local family
Larks View	2002-03	Bryant Homes/ Taylor Woodrow		Skylarks could be heard here!
Laura House, Jengers Mead	L 1980's			

Billingshurst's Heritage

Luggs Close	L 1990's			After Lugg's Yard which formerly stood there
Luxford Way	1999-2000	Taywood Homes	Penfold Grange Dev Phase 1	Local family, after Joseph Luxford
Manor Close	2012	Cross Construction	4 Eco homes sold before completion	After nearby Manor House
Maple Close	M 1960's			Tree Name
Maple Road	1970-71	Sunley Homes		Tree Name
Maplehurst Court, Brooker's Road	2002-03	Bellway Homes		After Maplehurst (Nuthurst Parish)
Mill Way	E 1960's	Horsham RDC		After former windmill
Morris Drive N	2002-03	Bryant Homes /Taylor Woodrow	Penfold Grange Dev Phase 5	Local family who lived at Five Oaks
Morris Drive S	1999-2000	Taywood Homes	Penfold Grange Dev Phase 1	Local family who lived at Five Oaks
Nightingale Walk	1978-80	Gleeson Homes		
Oaklands	L 1950's		Former garden of Broomfield Lodge	Refers to the 'Sussex weed'
Osmund Court, Rowan Drive	2006	Saxon Weald	40 Flats For The Elderly	
Ostlers View	1982	Hilbery Chaplin		
Pegasus Court, High Street	2002	Pegasus Retirement Homes PLC	Flats For The Elderly	From developer name
Petworth Court, Brooker's Road	2002-03	Bellway Homes		From Petworth town
Pine Close	M 1960's			Tree name
Platts Meadow	1998-99	Shared ownership	A plat is a small piece of land	
Pond Close	1998-99	Shared ownership		
Renton Close	1974-76	Sunley Homes		Local family prominent in local affairs
Roman Way	M 1990's	Shared ownership		Invaders' name
Rosehill - South	c.1970			After house that stood on site
Rosehill - North	c.1987-88			After house that stood on site
Rosier Way	L 1950's			After nearby wood
Rowan Court, Rowan Drive	L 1960's			Tree name
Rowan Drive	M 1960's			Tree name
St Gabriels Road	1978-80	Gleeson Homes		After Catholic church to the N
St Mary's Close	1988			After nearby Parish Church

132

Saddlers Close	2008-09	Barratt Homes/ Saxon Weald	Saddlery and leather craft was an important local industry	
Saville Court, Station Road	1972			After Saville House on the site
Saville Gardens, Station Road	1972		Formerly a row of terraced houses	
Saxon Close	M 1990's			Invaders' name
Silver Lane (South End)	E 1960's		Land owned by Puttocks, Clevelands	Silver Birches line the road
Silver Lane (North End)	M 1960's			Silver Birches line the road
Skylarks	2002-03	Bryant Homes/ Taylor Woodrow	Penfold Grange Dev Phase 5	Skylarks could be heard here!!
Stemp Drive	1974-76	Sunley Homes		Local family name
Sussex Court, Brooker's Road	2002-03	Bellway Homes		
The Alders	2011-12	Taylor Wimpey/ Saxon Weald	Alders Edge Dev (27 Properties)	Tree name
The Wadeys	1974-76	Sunley Homes		After local builder founded 1884
The Willows	2001-02	Taywood Homes	Penfold Grange Dev Phase 4	Tree name
Turner Avenue	2001-02	Taywood Homes	Penfold Grange Dev Phase 4	Turners buried in the Baptist Chapel Yard
Weald Court, Station Road	1973		Once the Whirlwind factory and Lorlins works	
Wicks Road	1974-76	Sunley Homes		Local name- Wally
Willow Drive	1970-71	Sunley Homes		Tree name
Windmill Place	2012	Devine Homes PLC		Development name - road name not yet allocated
Woodlands Way	L 1950's			Adjoins woodland

The following Appendices contain details from published Directories and other sources of people, places and businesses in Billingshurst from the Victorian years until the 1960s.

Appendix 2 The end of the Georgian years

The water mill wheel at Rowner Mill , William Carter, Miller

Pigot's Directory for 1832-4 states that 'Billingshurst's not remarkably productive. There are no manufactures unless that of tanning may be said under this head, of which there is one establishment'. The list of shopkeepers is shorter than 1839 but mentions Foice Champion, tea dealer, Richard Chennell, baker, Ann Miles, grocer, Phillip Puttock seedsman and grocer and James Turner, poulterer. The influence of the canal probably reflects the subsequent increase of trade. Most of the names quoted are still in office in 1839, but Cutfield & Co, Wharfingers are at Newbridge Wharf, Wm. Carter was a miller at Rowner water mill and Elijah Ford is also a miller. Maltsters are Maurice Farhall and William Towse. Stephen Evershed is called a farrier rather than a vetinary surgeon. Thomas Higgins is a currier [leather dresser] and Thomas Holman a tanner, Richard Mitchell is a carpenter, Luke Wadey a wheelwright and Henry Trower a gun and whitesmith [metal worker]. George Wells was then at the Kings Head, but he soon left for the Three Crowns at Wisborough Green. J.G.Read was the schoolmaster.

Clay, Wood, Leather, barley, wheat and iron are the basic raw materials of those making things in Billingshurst at the climax of the industrial revolution and who did not work on the land. These were the raw materials of self-sufficiency.

The railway had not yet arrived at the beginning of Queen Victoria's reign. When it came in 1859, it would open up great possibilities, as symbolised by all that was on show at the great Exhibition at Kensington in 1851. The introduction of parcel post in 1882 is often overlooked, but it facilitated national advertising of all the desirable new things being invented and marketed, all available by mail order from home and abroad. Victorian homes were notoriously cluttered with pictures and ornaments gathered from far afield.

Appendix 3
The early years of Queen Victoria

The Blacksmiths Arms, Adversane, today

Pigot's Directory of 1839 offered some interesting information. The fortnightly corn exchange meeting 'cannot properly be called a market'. Letters from London arrived by mail cart from Horsham every morning at five and were despatched every evening at ten. (The penny post began the following year). Rev Beath was the incumbent and there were 1,540 inhabitants.

John Napper of Maltham House was the Magistrate and George Wood of Summers was among the Gentry. William Boarer and Mary Voice ran day schools and Mary Medhurst also took in boarders, Peter Evershed was the surgeon and Henry Turner the Surveyor and Registrar of births and deaths. Matthew Caffin was land and timber surveyor and appraiser.

Fred Peskett ran The Blacksmiths' Arms, George Puttock the King's Arms and James Aylward the Kings Head.

[The close proximity of the two 'Kings 'pubs gave rise to the favourite jest of the 1660s. Charles Hindley in **Tavern Anecdotes** tells about a courtier of Charles II who asked a friend about a decent hostelry and was told, "You will find the King's Arms are always full while the King's Head is empty". The allusion is to Mistress Nell Gwyn.]

Shopkeepers and traders included John Allman, nursery and seedsman, David Baker, watchmaker, Wm. Brown, boot and shoemaker, two Carters at Adversane, blacksmith and grocer at Sayers and Edward Harwood, bootmaker, two Holdens, blacksmiths, Stephen Evershed, Vet., two Kensetts, butcher and grocer, draper and County Fire Office Agent, two Knights, grocer and maltster, three Lakers, tailors and hairdressers, currier and leather seller, Thomas Linfield, butcher, George Puttock, basket, sieve and hoop maker, Phillip Puttock, grocer, miller and nurseryman, James Puttock, fellmonger [dealer in skins] and glover, Thomas Puttock, grocer and draper, Wm Razell, saddler and shoemaker, Edward Robinson, butcher and grocer, Siward, Child and Henley, coal and lime merchants and barge owners, New Bridge Wharf, William Sprinks, miller, John Turner, lime burner and barge owner, New Bridge Wharf, two Voices, plumber and carpenter and boot and shoe maker and George Weller, boot maker.

The Comet coach from Bognor called at the King's Arms at a quarter to twelve every weekday to London via Dorking and Leatherhead. The return coach called at one, going via Pulborough and Arundel. The carrier, Levi Wade's **Waggon,** left for London every Monday. William King carried freight to Brighton and Guildford.

The picture here is of traders who made goods and provided services, rather than retailing items imported from further afield. The exceptions were groceries and clothing, doubtless brought in by the carriers. Georgian Billingshurst is largely self-sufficient.

An old photograph of the King's Head

Appendix 4 Mid-Victorian Billingshurst

Mill stone from the East mill used as a garden paving-stone at Hammonds

Melville's Directory of 1858 shows significant expansion, though little increase in population since 1839. Amongst the 'gentry' were Henry Carnsew at Gratwick House, Richard Denyer at Summers, John Ireland, Alfred Lloyd at Rowfold, Miss Ann Drinkwater, Thomas and Henry Baker, Charles Wonmer Ward and Joseph Kesterton at Great house. Rev Hugh Thomas was now Vicar, with a curate, Rev Cornwall. Rev. Leader was the 'Independent' clergyman.

Several names from twenty years earlier are still going strong. There are changes of landlord at the inns. Robert Bisshop was at the King's Arms Commercial Inn, licensed to let horses, Alfred Laker at the King's Head, and William Wood was a beer retailer at the Rising Sun, long since demolished. [This pub was opposite the Old Village Hall]. Edward Burchall was a retailer of beer as well as a grocer. Richard Mitchell combined building with brewing. Thomas Elliott was maltster and corn vendor. Strong drink mattered in Billingshurst! The brewing business required a resident Excise Officer to assess the tax; one was Peter Phillips and an earlier one, William Coulson.

David Baker, the watchmaker, had branched into building with his son, also David as plasterer and bricklayer. Henry King followed his father as carrier and Maurice Harwood too as bootmaker. Boots and leather goods also mattered. John Barnes, Albert Powell, William Streeter and William Voice were in the boot and shoe trade, and Caroline Puttock made gloves and gaiters. Jesse Laker was a currier. Another glover and dealer in wool was James Woods. Henry Laker made saddles, harness, rope and whips. The Puttocks were major players. John was a smith at the Blacksmiths Arms, Deborah a grocer and baker, Phillip a nursery and seedsman and Thomas a timber merchant. The Trower family too were significant traders. Mrs. Trower was a dressmaker, James a draper and grocer and William was a carrier to Horsham and Guildford. Other grocers were John Chart, also a draper and Insurance Agent, William Phillips, also a confectioner and baker and Peter Towse at the Five Oaks Inn. Peter Laker and James Turner were tailors. Others in the building trade were two William Wadeys, two Luke Wadeys, one a wheelwright and another James Turner. Other bakers and confectioners were Frederick Peskett and William Phillips. The butchers were Edward Robinson and William Grinsted. John Etherton and George Jupp were blacksmiths as well as John Puttock. [Deborah Evershed in her book about Adversane gives a warm account of a family Christmas party in 1856 at the home of George Puttock, wealthy timber merchant, in Billingshurst.]

William Boorer kept the academy and Miss Potter the seminary for young ladies. Evershed and son were surgeons, Stephen Evershed the Vetinary Surgeon.

Melville gives a useful list of mid Victorian farmers of the 5903 acres of productive land in Billingshurst as listed below:-

Thomas Barnes	Lordings
Thomas Botting	Oakhurst
William Bridger	Wood Dale
John Dean	Fewhurst
Thomas Evershed	Dunkins
James Evershed	Ridge
William Evershed	Tedfold
James Greenfield	Adversane, also mealman
William Gumbrill	
Thomas Ireland	
Walter Laker	Minses Wood
J. Meetens	Kingsfold
Hezekiah Miles	Soil Farm, Adversane
Charles Miles	Slinfold land
Henry Miram	Pratts
Charles Shepherd	Little Wood house
William Sprinks	also miller at Hammonds
Richard Towse	Hadfold, Adversane (married Sarah Miles 1807)
William Turner	Slatter
John Turner	Rosa

South Street before the building of the Women's Hall

Appendix 5 Late Victorian Billingshurst

Outside Dr. Hubert's surgery at Brick House, now the NatWest Bank

Kelly's Directory of 1880 illustrates changes of people and developments stimulated by the coming of the trains to the village. It lists the gentry as James Wilson living at Gratwicke House, Charles W. Schroeter at Tedfold, Maurice Ireland of Broomfield Lodge, Lord of the Manor of Bassett's Fee, The Duke of Norfolk K.G. of Pinkhurst. Henry Hurst, G.C.Gibson, Henry Puttock of Clevelands, Robert Goff of Summers Place, H.F.Locke-King, W.Berrall of Stanmore, F.A. Schroeter and James Wilson are the principle landowners.

Harvey Jupp collected the rates and taxes; Job Saunders Clark was the Postmaster, vintner and keeper of general stores, William Wood the Registrar and Relieving Officer, W. Simmons Station Master and Dr. W.H.Hubert Medical Officer and Public Vaccinator at Brick House. Arthur Dale was the Vet. Luxford and Harman were the carriers. Rev. H.L.Norden was the Vicar and the Rev. Lee was at the Congregational Church. Emma Chart had a day school and Miss Harriet Grinsted a school for young ladies. James Thornton was auctioneer and surveyor.

Forty individual householders are listed. These include Mrs Caffin at Station Road, four Eversheds and Edward Underwood at Hammonds House.

The 'Commercial' entries reveal how much more diverse the trade of the village had become towards the end of the 19th century. Grocers were numerous. Frank Arnold was at Churchgate, also a draper, John Blake at Five Oaks, Edwin Cork, also an outfitter, at Adversane, Job Clark, Frank Price, also a baker, Edward Standing at Newbridge, W.T. Voice, together with horses and traps in Station Road and Mr. Luxford. Clem Etheridge kept a shop and Thomas Gray was a general dealer.

There were other bakers: Elizabeth Green at Adversane and Joshua Rowland. Alfred Songhurst and Harry Foice were the butchers. There were three tailors, Edward Seller, Charles Reader and James Turner and Miss Eliza Allman was a dressmaker and William Cranham an upholsterer. Boot and shoemakers and dealers included Joseph Brown, William Hurst at Adversane, John Joyes at Andrews Hill, William Voice and Wagstaff and Son.

Other trade outlets included Miss Fanny Herrington, the stationer, John Mills the chemist and Edwin Gravett, the mealman. Walter Joyes had the corn, seed and coal and plumbing business at the Station. Services were provided by Alfred Mitchell, the carpenter, Edward Voice, the plumber, Harry Read, the chimney sweep, William Wadey wheelwright and smith, David Wadey builder and decorator and Walter Wadey, smith.

The building trade was active. Job Robinson was a general builder and contractor, Mrs Jane Wadey and sons were builders at Five Oaks. Ephraim Wadey, brickmaker and builder was at Parbrook. He owned the brickyard at Gilmans, south of Natt's Lane [in the Manor of Storrington!] from 1890 to 1913 when it was known as the Station Brickyard.

Other businesses were malting by George Constable, saddlery by Henry Laker and Son, leather goods by Walter Laker, timber and hoops by Henry Puttock and coopering by Joseph Hughes. Walter Weller sold coal from Station Road. William King dealt in poultry at Adversane.

Two people sold beer in off licences: Clem Matthews and Amelia Wood. At the pubs there were Mary Sprinks at the Station Inn, George Wooldridge at the Blacksmiths Arms, David Yarrow at the King's Head, James Towse at the Five Oaks Inn who also ran a shop and J. Butterworth Sisman at The King's Arms.

Farmers listed in 1890 include the following:

George Alvis	Lordings
George Bradford	South Eden
C.W. Schroeter	Jeffries
Mrs Joseph Cheesemere	Andrews Hill
John Evershed	Fewhurst
Henry Garton	Frenches
Owen Garton	Great Daux and Grooms
Robert Goff	Priors
Hugh Ireland	Manor House
George Ireland	High Fure
William Kennett	Hook Farm
Mrs Louisa Maas	Goldings Farm, Five Oaks
Mrs Charles Mills	Southlands, Adversane
Maurice Myram	Denhams
Mrs Elizabeth Sands	
Samuel Richardson	Five Oaks
William Steele	Palmers Farm
William Wells.	

Thomas Holland was steward to R. Goff and Thomas Burchell, bailiff to C.W. Schroeter.

Appendix 6

Early 20th century Billingshurst

1. R.Rhodes & Son in 1935, still going strong

2. R.Rhodes & Son in 2012, with Geoff Rhodes

The shops and businesses of Billingshurst are superbly illustrated in Wendy Lines' compilation of archive photographs in her book *'Billingshurst'* published in 1995. The following list is derived from that source, detailing people and premises from about 1900 to 1939. It serves as a useful record showing the continuity and the changes from Appendices 4 and 5. The information here is augmented from a booklet, 'Billingshurst and District' issued by Douglas Ross & Son, estate agents, auctioneers and valuers in the 1920s. Then as now the village shops were subject to frequent changes of use and of proprietor.

In 1925 F.A Skinner was the farmer at Cedars.

R. Rhodes & Sons (Cecil) Bootmakers, South Street.

The Parbook Nursery, Tea Gardens. Cakes, ices, fruit and flowers, wreaths, tomatoes and cucumbers cut to order.

At Oak Tree cottage on the A29 Miss Tucker sold sweets, lemonade etc. Open on Sundays.

Charles Tiller, Fruiterer and Confectioner was at The Rosary Tea House and Garden, Alick's Hill. Board residence offered and 'Printing of all descriptions'. He issued the *Billingshurst News Free Newspaper*.

R. Crisp Hairdresser, tobacconist, films developed. Wireless engineer, Agent for HMV gramophones and records. Accumulators charged for the wireless.

Cooter's Wood Oven Bakery off South Street. Cakes and pastries made on the premises, teas, tobacco and minerals. Jabez James Peay had the shop from 1911

The Crescent School, South Street.

Leonard V. Jarvis, The Pharmacy, High St. Agent for Kodak. Developing and printing.

E.&W. Cripps Family Butcher, High Street.

W.Ward, plumber, gas and hot water fitter, tinsmith, mowers repaired and ground. High St. Works.

W.H. Etheridge, haulage contractor, sweep, well sinker, sheep shearer and water diviner, East St.

King's Arms. Landlord John Butterworth Sisman (about 1910).

At the Six Bells Stephen Garmon was Landlord (1907)

Laker's Refreshment Rooms, High St., next door to old bank buildings.

Luxford's Shop was at the corner of East St, now a restaurant. At one time, a grocer, variously Balls, Butler and W.J.Barnes

The Post Office 1902 formerly where stood a low wall, fronting the High St. Job Saunders Clark was the Postmaster.

Mill Lane meadow is now the Library car park. A large barn once stood there.

Brick House. Dr W.H.Hubert's surgery, subsequently that of J.Croft, Vetinary Surgeon. Westminster Bank was built on the site of Brick House.

Rice Bros. High St. garage, 1926, then it became Southern Counties garage, now Budgens supermarket. 'Any make of car supplied'.

Field's Ironmongers, Crisp's Hairdresser, Tribe the butcher. All operated in what was the old Carlton House. Field gave way to Pilcher's, then R.S. Higgins and now Austin's. Serial ironmongers, 'Mowers, Valor oil stoves, Aladdin lamps etc.'

Tribe the butcher's first premises, then A.T.Jones the watchmaker, next the 15th century restaurant [now Monsoon Tandoori]. Tribe advertised, 'Our bacon is smoked on our own stoves. Families waited on daily within four miles'.

King's Head Landlords were variously J.Stewart and J.Howard Field.

Gingers House (Mediaeval) was still standing in 1930.

Gingers and the Maltings Hotel

The Maltings Hotel and tea gardens was converted in late 1920s from the original malt house.

The Malaya Garage was on the malting site, now demolished, stood at the entrance to Jengers Mead. It had earlier been Delaney's garage.[Now Truffles cafe].

The Rising Sun public house was opposite the old village hall, now demolished.

Whitehall was the Laker's home and leather shop, beside Rope Walk. (beside the present Roman Way).'Henry Laker, harness makers, bulk filtered petrol, footwear and shotgun cartridges'.

Whitehall garage (Alfred Laker).The house was demolished, the garage expanded. Now housing for the elderly.

The Manor House (of Bassett's Fee). A timber-framed building under a brick facade.

Old Village Hall 1906. Used by the community for meetings, whist drives, 'socials', dances, etc. until 1991, now converted to flats.

Gravett's Shop confectionary and bakery, now Oak Cottage.

John Argent's Shop, 1920s, grocer, baker, horse and trap for hire.

Bernard Baker, Draper and Outfitter, Argent's old place refurbished. 'If it's BB its good', footwear, shirts, corsets etc. Now Lloyd's Bank.

Queuing for a clothing sale at Baker's in 1949

Les Lusted's Shop, grocer and baker, High Street.

Voice's Monumental Works (19th century) demolished and rebuilt as Crisp's third shop. Part of the main house next door, became a florists.

Ben Moss, Fishmonger.' Fish sent direct from the coast, one day fresher than that sent to market'.

Churchgate, once a grocers, then a guest house, proprietor W.Cassie. Now an apartment.

Churchgate, East Street

Gordon Lugg's steam engine business, East Street.

W.T. Voice's shop, Station Road. Grocer, boots and shoes and Fly Proprietor. Just west of the railway. He was known as 'Bumper' Voice and carried passengers from the station to villages by horse and carriage.

Richard George had a General Store just east of the railway in the 20s and 30s, now Tescos He also had a butcher's shop opposite before Mr. Reynolds started his shop.

Malthouse, Station Road. James King owned that and the High St. plant.

Whirlwind Factory, on the malthouse site, now Weald Court flats.

The Railway Hotel (now Inn), Michell's Fine Ales. It has a new brick facade.

F.W. Watts, seed and corn merchants. End of Station Road. Formerly owned by Walter Joyes. It had silos and a mill building at the rear with its own siding for rail wagons. It finally closed in 1992.

1. F.W. Watts & Sons, Station Road

2. Hereford House

Hoop Sheds, near the Station. Henry Puttock, proprietor. Immediately behind Great Daux farmhouse. It also had rail access with an inspection pit.

Keating's Factory. Originally flea powder. Came from London to Daux Road in 1927. Now demolished.

Gas works built in 1907 off Natts Lane, demolished with advent of North Sea gas. In the 1950's people could buy coke for 7s-6d a bag.

Great Grooms at the corner of Natts Lane and Parbrook. Originally a farmhouse and barn, retitled Groomland Farm. Subsequently a restaurant and antiques business, but now residential again.

Hurstlands corner, opposite, had a single bungalow owned by Mrs. Strong. The fine stone boundary wall still stands beside the A29.

Fossbrooks was the home and original building premises of Ephraim Wadey.

Griggs, Old House, Southlands. Ancient hall houses at Adversane, older than The Blacksmiths Arms (1630) where Gaius Carley was the smith.

Old House was a restaurant and antique business. Now residential once again.

The Limeburners Inn at Newbridge. HQ of Billingshurst anglers fishing the Arun.

Newbridge warehouse, built 1839, now restored.

Rowner Lock, last used 1871. Restored 1982 by the Wey and Arun Canal Trust.

Rowner water mill. Demolished 1968.

Okehurst west of the village dated 1606.

Five Oaks Inn, built 1850, now demolished and used as a display area for a large Automobile firm, Harwood's of Pulborough.

Ingfield Manor built in 1909 by the Fielding family, owners of Okehurst. Since 1961 a school for children with cerebral palsy.

Five Oaks Farm. Morris family dairy farm. Robert Morris was first Chairman of The Parish Council, 1895.

Summers Place Convent School 1945 to 1984. Subsequently Sotheby's.

The Haven School in Slinfold Parish. Closed 1948 and demolished.

Charles E Wadey Builder, plumber and sanitary engineer. Office and works at Parbrook. The brickyard off Natts Lane was called Gillman's Brickyard. Burchell & Sons ran it from 1930 to 34, then Gillman's Brick Company from 1936.

The playing fields north of Natt's Lane were used by Billingshurst Football Club. They changed in dilapidated cattle sheds in the north east corner. It later became the recreation ground, housing the tennis club, the scout hut, a play school and the Horticultural Society's Flower show held in a marquee.

The Weald School site was open fields with a block of tumbledown corrugated iron farm sheds and a well, said to have been used as a slaughter house. It was demolished and taken to Itchingfield Refuse pit by the author and colleagues in the 1980s. The Junior School site was an open field, sometimes used for Bonfire Night. A line of superb elms lined the A29 on the east side. All were felled in 1974, ruined by Dutch Elm disease.

At the corner of the A272 and the A29 Mr. Coe had a second-hand shop, with Redman's coal yard behind it. There was also the wheelwright's shop and forge.

Duncan Reynolds has plotted the sequence of High Street shops as remembered in the 1950s. On the west side going north (towards Five Oaks) were 1.Mrs Whitehead's wool shop 2.International Stores 3. Chemist, Mr. Gillibrand 4 Higgins, Ironmongers 5 Mr. Cheal's butchers/fish shop 6 an alley way 7. Mr. Ward's sweet shop 8. A pair of cottages (Mrs.Lines).

Opposite on the east side going south were 1. Ware's the drapers 2. Alley 3. Bernard Baker's drapers 4. Lusted the bakers 5. Alley 6. Crisp's Wireless/barbers 7. Mr. Barnes dairy 8. Alley 9. Mr. Freeman's greengrocers 10 Mr. Trevelyan's shoe shop 11. William Voice's tobacconists 12. Mr. Myram's cafe 13. Westminster Bank

Appendix 7 Post WW II Billingshurst

Wally Wicks, Maj. Gen. Renton, Allan Dugdale of the Weald and John Sutton at the Horticultural Show, 1969

Many changes have occurred in the village shops and on the farms within the memory of people still in the land of the living. The following data derived from **Kelly's Directory (1962)** may serve as a reminder of days some fifty years ago. Where figures are given they refer to numbering in the High Street.

The magistrates on the Horsham Bench included General Renton of Rowfold, William Pemberton of the Manor House and Rudolph Fielding of Okehurst.

Rev. R. Evan Hopkins was Vicar and Rev. Gerard Candy the Catholic Priest, living at the Priest's Cottage in Lower Station Rd.

J.B. Sherlock of Renvyle, Oakhurst Rd. and R. Ayre of Bridgewater Farm were Rural District Councillors.

There were Post Offices with groceries at both Five Oaks kept by Mrs. Rogers and at Adversane by F. Sharville.

Victor Gee was Headmaster at the Weald Secondary Modern School and General Renton Chairman of Governors. On the Board of Governors was Mrs. Pamela Foster of Greatham, sometime secretary to the poet T.S. Eliot and direct descendant of William Wilberforce. She was later Chairman for many years.

The West Sussex County Library was housed at the Trinity Congregational Hall.

The Doctors were Bousfield, Hope-Gill and Tillyard at Churchgate. Miss Phyllis Bradley was a District Nurse and another, Nurse Baines lived in Chestnut Road. On the corner at The Lindens the Registrar of Births and Deaths attended one morning a week. J.Symmons was the dentist and A. Pasfield the Vetinary Surgeon.

A private school stood at the corner of Daux Avenue run by Mrs Murat.

Whitehead & Whitehead were the Estate Agents, amalgamated with D Ross & Son.

Garages included Hillview at 107, Malaya, Poplar, Rice Bros., Billingshurst Coaches (Williamsons Removals), Lawrensons Haulage at the Station, and Laker's petrol pumps. Fred Stenning sold bicycles and mopeds. A.G. Williams & sons were agricultural engineers at Frenches Corner and Gibbons in Daux Rd., R. Crisp 33/43 dealt in radios as did Radio Traders in Station Rd., L. Brown, electrical engineer, W.G. Keyte & sons, precision engineers in Daux Rd. and Keatings were manufacturing chemists. Mr. Lusted and Albert Collin ran taxis. There were no supermarkets but many grocers; International Stores 50, Co-op 41, R.& J. Ball 59, Fishers (with a PO) in Station Rd., Sidney Reynolds, Lower Station. Rd., Walker Stores 70 and E. Ross, mobile grocer. A.E.Hearne 71 and Mrs. Freeman 47 were greengrocers and there were High Seat Nurseries and J.H. Way's nursery at Little Platt, Marringdean Rd. too. L.K. Fisher 48, appropriately, was the fishmonger. The Misses Dance had a shop at 2 East St next door to Brick House as did Mrs. S. Jaegar at 89. Mrs. Whitehead was a draper at 58.

S.C.Reynold's shop, formerly a butchers, then a grocers, subsequently became a sub-post office and is currently an Asian take-away and a fish and chip shop. Next door were two other shops. Mrs. Lawrence was the draper, later a bookmakers. Shirley's cafe stood on the corner but was demolished when the Daux Road corner was widened. The cafe moved to where the Travelodge stands at Five Oaks. Opposite Reynold's was a newsagents run by Mr. And Mrs Fortune who kept Saluki dogs, then by the Shaws and next the Humphreys and finally Dillon's. It is now a Tesco Express.

S.C.Reynold's grocery shop in Lower Station Road

E.W.Cripps 82 and W.Tribe 50 were butchers. Mr. Cripps had his own abattoirs behind the shop. P. Reeves 85 was also a butcher.

R. Brown was the barber and ladies had a hairdressing choice of Palm Court in Station Road, Louise (Morris) 49 or Helene 126.

A. Cannon 42, L.&D. Morley 72 and A.J.Voice 53 were confectioners.

Alex Lochie 54 was the chemist and Sheila and S. Caton Ltd had a drug store in Lower Station Rd.

R.G Oulds of Daux Ave. was the photographer and there was a studio at 124. Watts by the Station sold corn and seeds and garden sundries. R.S. Higgins was the Ironmonger 31 and 52 with Higgins (Toys) at 55. T.Pearson 29 and J.Shaw of Lower Station Rd. were newsagents. R. Rhodes & Son 112 and C.Trevelyan 51 dealt in boots and shoes. Dairy products came from Express Dairies at the Station Yard [now Duplex Engineering] or Mrs. A. Voice at 45. Brush-Vac Services swept chimneys from Little East St. E. Carley did plumbing from Adversane and G. Carley was the last farrier left. Chas. Wadey & sons was the main builder at Parbrook. Gillman's Bricks Ltd. made them at Parbrook. Fred Voice offered building and plumbing services. William Mees was landlord at the Blacksmith's Arms, Peter Bowring at the Five Oaks Inn. H. Temple-Jones at the Six Bells offered hotel accommodation at 7 and a half guineas a week (£7.35p) and bed and breakfast for 15 shillings (75p).

151

Apart from the Pubs, refreshments could be taken at the Shirley Cafe (Woods) in Lower Station Rd. or Jane's Tea Garden at Five Oaks. The cafe site was later used for car sales and is now residential. There were neither take-away stores offering 'fast food' nor ethnic restaurants of any kind.

The main outfitter was Bernard Baker 37 and there was Patswear for Ladies (A. Maynard) in Lower Station Road and a dry cleaners was to be found in the High St.

Antiques were sold by B. Hawes-Wilson at Great Groomes and by M.M.Frame and Lola Baxter at Old House Restaurant, Adversane. Mrs. Thurlow-Smith 95 dealt in antique copper and brass.

A.C. Walker farmed at Stonepits, Marringdean Road. His widow, Aileen, did the pictures for the village signs and was made MBE for hers services to the village in 1998. Mr. Gordon Simkin designed the shields which stand beside the roads entering the village.

At the station there was a Station Master, two porters and the signal man who opened the crossing gates manually.

Gillmans Brickyard closed during WWII and was used as a rifle range. It was revived after the war but finally closed late in 1960. Bricks were handmade and stacked in clamps in open sheds next to Natts Lane. The sulphur fumes killed off most of the nearby trees.

Appendix 8
Occupants of Hammonds

Calms, diamond panes and old casement catches in window of Hammonds' attic

A synopsis of the people who occupied Cocksbrook, Hammonds and the mill as detailed in the main text:-

1327	John de Kockesbroke gave his name to Cocksbrook
1400	Wm Dakons (Daux) was paying for Cocksbrook
1530	Cocksbrook held by Greenfields
1557	Assigned to Richard West
1565	Francis Garton took a lease by copyhold on Cocksbrook
1581	Wm Lee holds a lease
1610	Wm Lee sold land to Edward Greenfield
1630	Anthony Haman I paid tax for Cocksbrook (m Susan Lee 1603)
1640	Anthony Haman I dies. Anthony II inherits Gilmans. Anthon II's brother Richard gets Cocksbrook when Anthony I's widow Susan I dies. Youngest sister is Susan II

1642	Richard Hammond holds Cocksbrook until 1680
1680	Anthony III inherits briefly
1682	Anthony III dies. Susan II, Richard's sister, inherits Hammonds
1685	Cow seized to pay Anthony III and Richard's debts.
1738	John Booker leases Cocksbrook. John Streeter pays Poor Tax
1767	Thomas Pacey had the lease and sold the freehold to John Streeter I
1779	Wm Streeter I pays Poor Tax for Hammonds and Cocksbrook
1795	Wm Streeter I dies, his widow inherits. His son Wm II gets Taintlands and Gingers. Wm III, James and John, grandsons, are to get the benefit of the sale when Wm II dies
1801	Wm II still paying tax on Taintlands, Gingers and Duckmore
1804	Wm II still at Hammonds but bankrupt
1806	Property alienated to farmer brother John Streeter II. Wm II fathers a natural son in the workhouse
1809	John Streeter II pays rent and Land Tax
1814	John II carting stone
1823	John II paying tax just for Hammonds House
1825	John Streeter II builds the mill. Richard Chennell is the miller
1827	Richard paying Poor Tax. Mrs. Evershed at Hammonds
1839	William Sprinks now the miller. John II still paying tithes
1850	John II dies having lived as a pauper. Daughter Mary Ann had married Thomas Trower. Wm Sprinks is a prospering farmer
1861	Wm Sprinks a widower at Hammonds
1867	Mary Ann Trower died. Her husband Thomas now owns Hammonds and Cocksbrook
1871	Sprinks still farming 140 acres, married to Ruth II
1874	H. Isted the miller
1878	W.F. Weller the miller
1881	Sprinks down to 26 acres
1881	Thomas Trower died. William Sprinks died and Edward Underwood now living at Hammonds
1891	Underwood still there – died 1923
1906	The mill cap blown off
	Early 20th century – the Trowers are at Hammonds
1920	All smock of mill gone, burnt. Base used as a store
1966	Mary Trower dies ages 82
1968	Gertrude dies aged 77, Hammonds auctioned off.
1969	Dr. Kilsby owns it
1983	John Griffin occupant.

Index

In addition to the names of people and places referred to in the main text about thirty other proper names found only in the appendices are included in the index. However many other references to people and places in the appendices are omitted for the sake of brevity.

Act of Uniformity, 30, 90
Adur, 6
adze, 24
Aella, 12
Albury, 30
Alfold, 16
Alfoldean, 9
Alfred the Great, 13, 23
Allman, 102, 136, 141
Alwyn, 60
Anderida Forest, 7
Andredesweald, 25
Anglo-Saxon Chronicle, 13
Arnold, 85, 100, 141
Arun, 3, 6, 19, 68, 103, 129, 148
Arundel, 13, 14, 17, 29, 30, 41, 46, 68, 124, 129, 137
Ashington, 25, 117
assart, 25
Atrebates, 6
Augustine, 22
aurochs, 3
Ayling, 102
Aylward, 74, 83, 136
Baker, 64, 74, 76, 120, 136, 138, 145, 146, 150, 154
Baptist Chapel, 60, 74, 75, 94, 133
Barclays, 52
Barnes, 20, 21, 116, 127, 138, 139, 144, 150
Barralets, 93
barrel drain, 6
Bartellot, 29, 32
Bartholomew, 30, 35, 42, 59, 66
Bassett's Fee, 25, 29, 46, 62, 141, 145

Bassetts Fee, 32, 40, 42, 57, 62, 100
Baxter, 120, 154
Beath, 32, 74, 136
Beck, 87, 100, 120, 125
Bede, 25
Beedings Castle, 2
beehouse', 52
Belgae, 7, 9
Bell Cottage, 64, 65
Beowulf, 13
Bettesworth, 62
Bignor, 9, 11
Bishopp, 75
Black Death, 26, 38
Blackpatch, 4
Blacksmith's Arms, 34, 153
Blue Idol, 124, 125, 127
Boarer, 74, 136
Bonfire, 48, 112, 120, 148
Booker, 57, 58, 59, 61, 156
Botting, 30, 139
boute coupe, 2
Bowling Alley, 6, 87, 90, 98, 104, 110, 118
Boxgrove, 1
Bramber, 14, 28, 29
Braose, 14, 29
Brereton, 32
Bretwalda, 15
Brick House, 31, 32, 101, 102, 141, 144, 152
Bridger, 71, 139
Bridgewater, 80, 129, 151
Brinsbury, 103, 105
Bristow, 103
Bronze Age, 5

Broomfield Lodge, 93, 132, 141
Broomfields, 43, 57
Budgens, 83, 93, 98, 144
Buffaloes, 53
Bull, 32, 88
Bungar, 47
Burchell, 90
Buttery, 50, 51
Caedwalla, 13
Caffin, 74, 102, 136, 141
Caffyn, 60, 102
Candy, 115, 151
Cannon, 153
Canute, 23
Carley, 148, 153
Carlton, 98, 100, 144
Carnsew, 32, 62, 85, 88, 90, 120, 138
Carpenters, 31, 98, 129
Carter, 13, 65, 74, 92, 100, 110, 120, 135
Catshill, 56, 62
Causeway, 32, 114
Celtic, 6, 9, 13
Celts, 7
Ceorl, 13
Champion, 7, 18, 25, 59, 80, 135
Chanctonbury, 7, 113
Chantler, 65
Charcoal, 21
Charman, 48, 60
Chart, 100, 138, 141
Chaucer, 14, 17, 43
Chennell, 70, 71, 135, 156
Chesemans, 46
Chichester, 1, 6, 9, 12, 14, 16, 24, 29, 40, 42, 130
Chime, 90, 110
Churchgate, 31, 100, 110, 141, 146, 147, 152
Cissbury, 4, 7
Clear, 42, 90
Cleveland House, 112
Clevelands, 3, 98, 101, 107, 114, 130, 132, 141
Clock Field Charity, 34
Cobbett, 70, 71
Cocksbrook, 6, 20, 21, 25, 41, 43, 47, 48, 59, 61, 62, 66, 84, 119, 123, 155, 156

Cogidumnus, 9
Coleman, 102
Collins, 42
Comet, 71, 82, 137
Coneyhurst, 13
Congregational Church, 89, 141
Constantine, 11
Convent, 62, 86, 148
Coolham, 10, 67, 105, 124, 125
Coombe, 77, 130
Coombes, 100
Coombs, 120, 121
Cooper, 13, 57, 101
Cooter, 143
Coppicing, 21, 92
copyhold, 40, 46, 155
Cordwood, 21
Cork, 141
Corn Laws, 20
Couchers, 119
Coulson, 138
Cowan, 75
Cowfold, 67
Craft, 101
Cranham, 130, 141
Cripps, 114, 120, 143, 153
Crisp, 78, 100, 120, 143, 144, 146, 150, 152
Croft, 98, 144
Cro-Magnon, 2
Croucher, 90
Crouchers, 43, 44
Crutchlow, 54
Dakons, 43
Danelaw, 23
Daux Wood, 3, 7, 130
Dawkes, 43
Dawks, 57
dinosaurs, 4, 67
Doggerland, 3
Domesday Book, 12
Downes, 30
Drove Roads, 16, 18
droving roads, 10
Druids, 6
Drungewick, 16

156

Duckmore, 29, 56, 62, 66, 90, 116, 119, 156
Duke of Norfolk, 42, 74, 100, 141
Durham, 89
Easton, 120, 130
Easwrith, 41, 43, 77
Edis, 32
Enfield, 120
Ephraim, 100, 115, 142, 148
Ethelred, 23
Etheridge, 141, 144
Evershed, 32, 44, 60, 66, 70, 74, 76, 89, 102, 127, 135, 136, 139, 142, 156
Ewins, 83, 95
Fallow, 19
falod, 16
Family Church, 124
Farhall, 74, 90, 135
Fecamp, 29, 42
Ferring with Fure, 16, 40
Fielding, 148, 151
Fire Station, 105, 122
Fishbourne, 9, 10
Five Oaks, 10, 20, 33, 76, 79, 82, 86, 100, 120, 123, 131, 132, 138, 141, 142, 148, 149, 151, 152, 153
Flight, 64
flint mines, 4
Foice, 80, 98, 100, 135, 141
Forge Way, 107, 108, 130
Franklin, 14
Friendly Societies, 52
Frye, 29
Fuller, 32, 60, 73, 76
Fuste, 48
Garton, 42, 46, 142, 155
Gas, 92, 99, 103, 104, 147
Gillmans, 142, 154
Gilmans, 54, 68, 104, 129, 155
Gingers, 63, 66, 131, 144, 145, 156
Glebe Land, 30
Goff, 62, 92, 100, 120, 141, 142
Goodyer, 95
Gore Farm, 64, 65
Gore Farm house, 64, 65
Gorefield, 47

Goring, 29, 30, 32, 36, 74, 88, 90, 120
Gratwick, 57, 60, 72, 90, 95, 97, 100, 101, 107, 114, 138
Gratwicke, 56, 101, 104, 110, 116, 130, 141
Gravatt, 102
Gravett, 120, 142, 145
Great Daux, 6, 44, 45, 66, 142, 147
Great Grooms, 148
Greenfield, 13, 29, 44, 56, 57, 59, 60, 65, 72, 139, 155
greensand, 2, 7, 16, 18
greenstone axe., 3
Griffin, 109, 120, 127, 130, 156
Groomsland, 104, 131
Hadfolds-herns, 19
Hammers, 5
Hammonds, 19, 41, 44, 48, 49, 53, 62, 64, 66, 80, 109, 116
Hardham, 9, 24
Harold, 24, 115
Harrow Hill, 4
Harwood, 74, 136, 138, 148
Haywards, 78
Head, 100, 136
Henshaw, 30, 32, 42, 48
heptarchy, 14
heriot, 38, 59
Hide, 39
hides, 13, 39
Higgins, 135, 144, 150, 153
Hill House, 90
Hill View, 83
Hilland, 48
Hilton, 30
Hoile, 69, 94
Holmes, 105
hominids, 1
Homo sapiens, 1, 2, 3
Hope-Gill, 117, 152
Horsham, 12, 19, 33, 57, 61, 71, 75, 79, 90, 109
Horsham stone, 44, 49, 67, 116
Hubert, 31, 101, 102, 103, 120, 122, 141, 144
Huberts, 100
Hughes, 60, 72, 74, 115, 142
Huguenot, 47

157

Humphreys, 120, 152
Hundred, 39, 43, 77
Hurd, 43, 127
Hurst, 13, 141
Hurstlands, 131, 148
Ingfield Manor, 86, 105, 148
Ireland, 42, 74, 89, 98, 100, 102, 112, 120, 138, 139, 141, 142
Iron Age, 6, 7
Isted, 94, 156
Itchingfield, 33, 48, 148
Jeavons, 87
Jefferies, 102
Jengers, 6, 63, 90, 107, 131, 145
Jengers Mead, 90
Johnson, 13, 66, 69, 73, 80
Jones, 120, 144, 153
Joyes, 142, 147
Jubilee Fields, 21, 108, 112, 115, 122
Keating's, 93, 147
Kensett, 60, 74, 102, 136
Keyte, 152
Kilsby, 109, 156
King, 93, 138, 142, 147
King, the maltster, 93
Kings Arms, 30, 53, 70, 71, 74, 78, 90, 102, 136, 137, 138, 142, 144
Kings Head, 73, 74, 82, 102, 135, 136, 138, 142, 144, 145
Kingsfold, 16, 104, 131, 139
Kitchener, 118
Knepp, 28
Knight, 14, 17, 41, 48, 74
Kockesbroke, 43, 155
Laker, 98, 102, 127, 138, 139, 142, 144, 145, 152
Lakers, 74, 120, 131, 136
Land Tax, 63, 67, 69, 71, 102, 156
Langley, 74
Leaman, 120
Lee, 47, 48, 141, 155
Leyland, 62
Limeburners, 116
Lines, 86, 93, 127, 143, 150
Lintott, 95
Lions, 122

Little Daux, 69, 116, 117
Lloyds Bank, 12, 52, 102
Lockyers, 48, 56, 60, 72, 74, 80, 90, 110
Longhurst, 102, 120
Lordings, 92, 139, 142
Luggs, 108, 109, 110, 131
Lusted, 120, 146, 150, 152
Lutyens, 97
Luxford, 32, 95, 98, 101, 107, 120, 131, 141, 144
Magna Carta, 28
Maille, 105, 114
Malaya, 83, 145, 152
malt houses, 20
Malt Tax, 53
Maltings Hotel, 123, 145
maltster, 57, 74, 93, 101, 102, 136, 138
maltsters, 19, 52
Manor House, 25, 34, 42, 100, 131, 142, 145, 151
Marcus Aurelius, 10
Marringdean, 26, 67, 79, 86, 98, 104, 114, 152, 154
merchet, 38
Merrikin, 120
Mesolithic, 3
Michell, 75, 147
Miles, 76, 135, 139
Mill Barn, 74, 115, 116
Mill Way, 64, 131
Mitchell, 102, 135, 138, 142
Montgomery, 14, 41
Moreton, 87, 120
Morris, 20, 33, 64, 120, 127, 131, 132, 148, 153
Murat, 86, 152
Napoleonic wars, 19
Natts Lane, 6, 131, 147, 148, 154
Neanderthal, 1, 2
Neolithic, 3, 4
New Road, 62
Newbridge, 12, 19, 60, 62, 98, 131, 135, 141, 148
Newpound, 92, 110
Norris, 97, 98, 100, 101, 110, 116, 120
North Heath, 87, 123
Noviomagus Reginorum, 9

Nutbourne, 2
Nye, 54
Odin, 12
Okehurst, 3, 29, 32, 148, 151
Old House, 44, 148, 154
Old Pratts, 62
Old Reservoir Farm, 104
Old Village Hall, 99, 112, 122, 138, 145
Old Workhouse, 47, 59
Oram, 30, 102
Orkneys, 3
Pacey, 61, 156
Palaeolithic, 1
pannage, 16, 17
Parbrook, 6, 100, 104, 142, 148, 153
Parish Chest, 35, 127
Parish Council, 36, 87, 102, 103, 107, 120, 122, 125, 127, 130, 148
Parish Room, 52, 78
Pasfield, 152
Patterson, 100, 120, 127
Paul Smith, 114, 127, 129
Peacock, 95
Pearson, 153
Penfold, 30, 54, 129, 130, 131, 132, 133
Peskett, 74, 136, 139
Petworth, 25, 30, 66, 78, 79, 132
Pevsner, 32, 61, 65, 114, 119
Phillips, 112, 138, 139
Pinkhurst, 25, 40, 41, 42, 55, 58, 61, 62, 66, 79, 84, 94, 100, 141
Pleistocene, 1
Police Act, 77
Poll Tax, 38
Poor Law, 36, 47, 71, 72, 78
Poor Tax, 34, 36, 59, 60, 62, 66, 69, 70, 71, 156
posnets, 50
Pulborough, 2, 9, 12, 103, 115, 116, 126, 137, 148
Puttock, 60, 72, 74, 83, 89, 92, 98, 100, 112, 122, 135, 136, 138, 139, 141, 142, 147
Quaker, 30, 35, 124, 125
Quick's, 98
Railway Hotel, 75, 147
Railway Inn, 75, 76, 83

Read, 135, 142
Reeve, 14, 42
Renolds Totham, 68
Renton, 32, 96, 98, 100, 111, 120, 132, 151
Reynolds, 127, 147, 149, 152
Rhodes, 53, 105, 106, 107, 120, 127, 143, 153
Rice Bros, 98, 144, 152
Richard, 29, 120, 121
Rising Sun, 138, 145
River Arun, 6, 129
Robin, 90, 91, 110
Robinson, 66, 136, 139, 142
Rose Hill, 100
Rosehill, 31, 101, 102, 108, 129, 132
Rosier, 29, 105, 132
Ross, 127, 143, 152
Rotary, 122
Rowfold, 6, 16, 25, 32, 69, 79, 89, 96, 98, 100, 111, 112, 138, 151
Rowfold Grange, 6, 32, 96, 100, 111, 112
Rowner, 1, 12, 120, 135, 148
Royal Observer Corps, 104
Rudgwick, 26, 57
Sadler, 90
Scats, 12, 93
School Lane, 85, 108, 117
Schroeter, 100, 141, 142
Selsey, 24
serfs, 16, 17, 38, 40
shaws, 18, 19, 21, 26
Shelley, 48, 75
Shepherd, 98, 110, 120, 139
Shepley, 100
Sherlock, 151
Shipley, 19, 80
Shirley, 152, 154
Silver Lane, 68, 107, 113, 132
Simkin, 154
Slinfold, 16, 21, 25, 139, 148
Smart, 60
Somer, 61
South Down, 17, 18
Southlands, 15, 142, 148
Speenhamland, 63, 72
Sprinks, 49, 74, 75, 76, 80, 83, 90, 94, 95, 137,

139, 142, 156
St. Gabriel's, 87, 114
St. Mary's, 28, 33, 35, 46, 61, 64, 67, 74, 88, 92, 97, 109
Stammerham, 67
Stane Street, 9, 10, 16, 67, 129
Stanley, 98, 99, 100
Star, 102
Stedman, 42
Stiles, 93, 98, 120
Stone, 1, 3, 67, 115, 131
Storrington, 25, 40, 42, 100, 127, 142
Streater, 59, 61, 62, 63, 64, 66, 67, 69, 71
Streeter, 49, 66, 67, 70, 74, 79, 84, 98, 138, 156
Stringer, 54
Summers Place, 6, 61, 62, 85, 86, 90, 100, 114, 141, 148
Sussex Cattle, 18
Sussex Marble, 67
Sussex Weed, 7
Swing, 71
Syon, 29, 42
Taintland, 63, 64, 66, 156
Tate, 35, 127
Tedfold, 76, 105, 139, 141
ten steps, 98
Tesco, 93, 152
Teulon, 81
Thakeham, 30
Thomas de Selhurst, 29
Tidy, 80
Tillyard, 152
Tipping, 42
Tithe cottage, 114
Tithes, 29, 35, 36, 37
Tithing, 39
Tower's, 59
Townland, 34
Towse, 59, 76, 135, 138, 139, 142
Trevelyan, 127, 150, 153
Tribe, 144, 153
Trower, 30, 69, 76, 79, 84, 94, 109, 135, 138, 156
Trundle, 6
Turner, 60, 65, 74, 114, 133, 135, 136, 137, 138, 139, 141
Turnpike, 82
Underwood, 94, 95, 141, 156
Union, 78, 79
vacuum, 83, 98
Vestry, 32, 34, 35, 36, 37, 61, 68, 76, 77, 78
Vicarage, 30, 35, 59, 80, 81, 98, 100
Vill, 24, 39
Village Green, 32, 114
villeins, 40
Vine Cottage, 64, 65
Virgate, 39
Voice, 20, 64, 74, 80, 88, 104, 136, 138, 141, 142, 146, 147, 150, 153
W.G.Grace, 92
Wadey, 74, 83, 88, 98, 100, 115, 120, 130, 135, 142, 148, 153
Walker, 98, 152, 154
War Memorial, 122, 123
Ward, 138, 143, 150
Ware, 98, 150
Watts, 120, 147, 153
Weald Court, 93, 107, 133, 147
Weald School, 85, 88, 100, 101, 108, 111, 122, 148
Weller, 94, 137, 142, 156
Wells, 30, 76, 80, 89, 120, 135, 142
West, 21, 25, 33, 46, 47, 98, 102, 127, 129, 130, 155
West Chiltington, 16, 21, 25, 33
West Street, 89
Westminster, 31, 52, 94, 102, 144, 150
Weston, 57
Whirlwind, 93, 105, 133, 147
White Horse, 102
Whitehall garage, 145
Wicks, 120, 133, 151
Wiggonholt, 25, 40
Wildens, 68, 98
Wilfrid, 22
William the Conqueror, 24, 41
Wilson, 30, 83, 90, 95, 131, 141, 154
Winklestone, 46
Wisborough Green, 3, 10, 33, 47, 124, 127, 135

Women's Hall, 122, 125, 126, 140
Women's Institute, 122, 125, 127
Wooddale, 6, 65, 100, 105
Working Men's Club, 86, 95, 96, 98, 120
Worsfold, 75
Wray Brown, 34
Wright, 13, 32, 86, 95, 120
Wylde, 120
Young, 18, 19, 127

Billingshurst's Heritage

CPSIA information can be obtained at www.ICGtesting.com
Printed in the USA
LVOW021124271212

3268LVUK00004B/4/P